ISBN **978-1-943159-09-3**

LCCN 2018949276

The publisher would appreciate notification where errors occur so that they may be corrected in subsequent printing and/or editions. Please send comments to the publisher by emailing to <u>deeprivers67@yahoo.com</u>

Printed in the United States of America

Dedication page

I dedicate this book to my family, mainly the three most important people in my life.

My first born Ralph M. Edgerson III, son you have made me into a better man. My only wish is to show you perfection in the hope that you become better than I could ever imagine.

To my Princess Bryanna Nykolé Edgerson, I love you more than you will ever know and you are truly destined for great things baby girl.

To my rib, my soul, my air, my everything Darlene D Edgerson, you have supported me from day one. From days of riding the bus with backpacks on to laughing at each other in our home.

I watermelon you baby!

2

DECISIONS...

By: Ralph M. Edgerson Jr

CHAPTER 1

Sitting at his desk, finishing up his last invoice. Cedric

Daniels just noticed that his 30 day vacation is about to start in 15

minutes. Glancing out of his office door, looking at the people he

won't see for a month and thinking about all the peace and

relaxation that's on it's way. The phone rings, "No not now",

Cedric muttered. Answering the phone in an Executive voice,

"Orleans Parish Medical...Daniels speaking how can I help you?"

"Hello. How can I help you?" The sweetest voice comes over the

phone, "Hey baby, you getting ready to leave?" Denise Daniels,

Cedric's wife on the phone waiting for a response. "Yup, shutting

5

down my computer as we speak", responds a smiling Cedric. "Well you know you gotta come and pick me up on your way home", Denise saying quickly out of her mouth. With a pause of everything Cedric wondered why he has to go 20 minutes in the other direction of his house. To pick up his wife from her job.

"What's wrong with your car?", Cedric quietly asked. Hoping she doesn't give her usual drawn out talks about why can't he just do what she ask of him. Denise simply replies, "Baby you forgot that I had to drop the car off at the Mechanic?" "Oh my bad, it slipped my mind.", replied Cedric. "Well let me finish up and I'll be there shortly" Cedric stated while reaching for his last print outs of today's work load. "Bye baby!", hanging up the phone quickly Cedric heads out of his office and to the garage where his truck was parked. As Cedric headed to the elevator that leads to the garage. He noticed grumpy, uncomfortable, and disgruntled employees looking at him with envy. Cedric just waived at everyone saying goodbye to those who really matter to him. When Cedric got close to his shiny black suburban he was startled by the click clack of a woman's high heels. 'Click, clack'. There it goes again. A soft seductive voice fills up the echoing garage, "You leaving me?" When Cedric turned around there stood a 6 foot 1 inch athletic thick frame of his co-worker Sherell White. Cedric and Sherell been co-workers for 13 years, longer than he and his wife been together. In those 13 years Sherell has been having a crush on Cedric for more than 7 of those years. Cedric knowing that never really went any further than just a platonic friendship. In his mind, "you never mix work and love". As much as he wanted to break that rule he denied himself that pleasure. Asking Sherell in a joking way, "Wha cha want?" Sherell replied in her usually soft voice, "You." Cedric stunned with a gaped open mouth, "Uh, what do you mean?" "I'm clowning with you man. You can't take a joke?", Sherell suddenly replied with the cutest little smile. Knowing in the back of her mind she wished he would have said. "me too." "You leaving without giving me my goodbye hug", she said. "Oh my bad girl, a brotha gotta go and pick up your friend from work." Sherell knowing exactly who Cedric is talking about just replied, "Oh ok." Giving Sherell a tight hug like you would a cousin you haven't seen in a while. Sherell melted in Cedric's arms quicker than ice on a Houston's summer sidewalk. Before she could even exhale in ecstasy, Cedric's cell phone rings. "Oh, I gotta get this", said Cedric. While he was on the phone Sherell stood next to him like a little puppy waiting for some affection from their master. "Hey, what's happening man. Sitting here talking to Sherell in the garage. Where you at? C'mon it's not like that." Cedric closing his cell turned and told Sherell, "That was Kevin, you know Kevin Talport. He's on the next level coming down and wanted to tell me bye. Like I'm not coming back in a month." Sherell smiles and replies, "You're just a liked person Ced. People tend to just like you automatically."

You can hear the engine before you see it turn the bend. Plus if you're a muscle car man you fall in love with the vehicle the first time you see it's racing strips, dual mufflers, loud 405 engine block, and candy apple red paint job. A 1973 Chevy Nova in mint condition, speeding through the garage, and heading straight toward Cedric and Sherell. "Here comes Kevin", Cedric stating with a look in his eyes like a kid seeing Spiderman in person. Kevin was a young exec who really doesn't have to work. Being the son of the Chairman of the Board of Directors for one of the largest Medical Institutes in Louisiana and Mississippi. Kevin felt more comfortable around working class people than what he called, "stuck-up, anal tension, snobs". The "rich and famous" is what we call them. "What's up peoples!", said Kevin with a smile on his face bigger than the cat in that "Alice in the Wonderland" book. "Just chillin man, getting ready to race up outta here" said Cedric with a grin. Opening up the trunk of his car Kevin turned to Cedric and said, "How bout a brew before you 'race...outta here' man. Sherell you want one?" "No I gotta get back and finish up some work that I left on my desk, just telling Ced bye before he leaves for his vacation", she replied. "Well I guess I'll talk to you later uh?" Sherell said in a wanting voice. Thinking nothing of it Cedric just responded, "Yeah baby girl yeah." Sherell walked off sexier than she did when she walked up to Cedric. Making every step fiercer than before, like she was a model on a runway. As she entered the elevator doors Sherell turned and took one more look at her crush. Then focused on Kevin and rolled her eyes as the elevator doors closed. "Man if that girl ain't loving on you, I don't know what to call it", stated Kevin as he popped open two bottles of beer. "Man go 'head on with that, me and her are strictly friends and that's it", replied Cedric thinking back to when he and Sherell, at the young age of 18, first started working together. He and Sherell started as file clerks for the Medical Center. Working late hours to make ends meet and try to keep from living pay check to pay check. Sherell being a single mom to a bouncing baby boy had more than her mouth to feed, while Cedric a bachelor was just trying to make his crib just a little more extravagant. They always seemed to work well and late together, she would sort out the files and he would file it all in. One late night Sherell took it upon herself to massage Cedric's shoulders while he was putting some files away and he didn't want her to stop, in fact Cedric leaned back into Sherell's chest. They both were very aroused but Cedric's rule came into play, "You never mix work and love" and that was the end of that. "Hello! You in there?" shouted Kevin. "I'm just saying the peach is ripe and ready to be picked, you just ain't bitin' are you?" said Kevin with a confused look on his face. Cedric replied, "Dude I'm married and I love my wife, besides you never mix....". And that's when Cedric remembered he had an appointment to keep, "Shit! My wife I was supposed to go get her!" Cedric jumped in his black SUV and handed Kevin a half-full bottle of beer. "Go ahead man, hit me up later", Kevin replied. As Cedric sped off thru the garage to the main street, Kevin realized that his buddy Ced dropped his cell phone when he rushed into the truck. Kevin tried to flag Cedric down but to no avail. Cedric sped down busy Tulane Avenue which is known for having traffic even at 12 o'clock in the afternoon. He hurried up and merged on the traffic filled Interstate 10 heading east, thinking aloud to himself, "Man I'm bout to hear her mouth. Let me call her and let her know what's going on..." That's when he noticed he couldn't find his cell. "Where is it?" He frantically

looked for the missing phone while also trying to pay attention to

slow driving drivers, sleepy truck drivers, and errand running

moms on the road. "Dammit! Where could it be? I just had it in

my hand" , Cedric thought. Brushing the dilemma off Cedric

focused on getting to his wife who was expecting him any minute

now and knowing he was at least 15 minutes from being even

close to her. Cedric and Denise been together for 5 years and was

married for 3 of those years. Being newlyweds and both being

married for the first time has it's ups and downs, even though they

both love each other dearly. Cedric and Denise both have their

faults and down falls, but they always seem to work their

problems out.

Cedric met Denise at the mall 6 years ago, he saw this woman

standing in front of a kids store and couldn't help his self but to go

and talk to her. At the time all Cedric could see was this healthy 5

foot 2 "red-bone" female with full luscious lips, thighs the size of a thoroughbred, a small waist, and breast that demanded you to look at them. He walked up to her and simply extended his hand and said, "Hi, my name is Cedric Daniels. I'm not crazy but I just had to come over and speak to you. I've never seen a model just chill in the mall without an entourage following her." "Model?", she replied laughing, "no not me you must be thinking of someone else baby." Denise looked over this 6 foot 5 "dark chocolate" man standing in front of her and couldn't help but to notice the massive arms exiting out of his crisp white t-shirt, his masculine solid chest, and not to mention the freshly manicured full beard framing out his million dollar smile. The ice was broken and they were friends first and it just grew into a strong relationship.

As Cedric pulled into the Michoud NASA Center parking lot he didn't see Denise outside waiting for him. Cedric exhaled a sigh of relief. When he stopped in front of the building Denise and the front desk security guard Jamal walked out. As she entered the truck Denise waived off the patrolling guard with a smile and closed the door. Cedric started apologizing immediately, "Baby I'm so sorry for being so late." Denise turned and looked at Cedric with so much disgust in her eyes and just replied, "What took you so long! I have been out there waiting for about 40 minutes like an ass!" "Baby I got side tracked for a minute. Sherell and Kevin wanted to tell me bye before I left for my vacation.", he replied pitifully. Sarcastically responding to his excuse Denise simply said, "Oh your girlfriend wanted to tell her man bye?" Mumbling under her breathe, "That bitch really working on my nerves." Cedric heard her say something but couldn't tell what it was. "Baby it's not like that. You making something out of nothing", pleaded Cedric. As Denise was getting ready to respond to what Cedric had just said. Her cell phone began ringing. She answered the phone and Sherell was on the other end, "Hey Denise, this Sherell White, I was calling you so you could let Cedric know he dropped his cell phone in the garage. Kevin brought it to me cause he figured I would know how to get in touch with you people."

Denise with the fakest of smiling voices replied, "Oh ok girl I'll tell'em." Then she just hung up the phone and turned to her husband and now sarcastically telling him, "You left your phone with your bitch! Next time make sure you got all of your shit before you leave her and come by me!" Cedric now turned and looked at Denise highly upset in a very stern voice, "What the hell are you talking about! Me and the girl are friends and friends only. I'm really getting sick and tired of you accusing us of messing around." "I don't wanna hear that shit! You and that bitch always talking. Every time I pass by your job either the bitch coming out of your office or she always in my face with her 'bobble-head' ass smiling and shit.", Denise shouting back at him. "The fucking girl likes you! She trying to be friends with your dumb-ass!", shouted back Cedric. "That bitch likes you and you know it. Don't play me for no fool Ced. Cause I'm not falling for your bullshit!",responded Denise. Cedric quietly and simply replied, "I'm really not in the mood for this shit. I'm tired of listening to it." "Oh you ignoring me now, well fuck you too

BITCH!", replied Denise. Cedric started thinking how did this go this far, he knew being late couldn't be this drastic and why was his wife this mad over him picking her up late from work. He wanted to ask but looking over at his wife's arms folded, leg shaking, and her eyebrows balled-up in the middle of her eyes he knew not to say a word and the truck stayed quiet the rest of the way home.

Riding down their neighborhood street Denise began collecting her designer purse, her lunch container, and some work she brought home that needed finishing up. Before Cedric could even put the big suburban in park she exited the vehicle and slammed the door. All Cedric could do is shake his head in confusion over what he felt was a situation blown out of proportion. While slamming the door to their house Denise locked the door, just by habit. When Cedric got to the door and found it locked a spark went off in him that ignited a fire never seen by his wife in the 6 years they've known each other. Cedric took one step back and with a force only seen on police videos or an action packed cop movie, he kicked the door in with such impact it came off it's hinges. Denise turned and screamed in horror thinking the worst but only encountered Cedric yelling at the top of his lungs, "Who the fuck do you think you are? I don't know what's the matter with your ass but I advise you to fix it dammit." Denise seeing the devastation that her husband just made did what most scared people do and backed down and away from the problem but as Cedric committed to his advancements toward his wife she then did what most scared people do when cornered. She attacked, striking Cedric in the face with an open-hand slap then administering the worst pain that would drop any man by kicking him square between his legs as hard as she can. Cedric's "Self-defense classes" he paid for finally paid off. Responding to his yelling Denise simply replied in the calmest of voice "Have you lost your fucking mind? Nigger you just kicked in my fucking door. Get the fuck out. GET THE FUCK OUT!!" Cedric gathered up the last bit of manhood he had left, turned around, and walked out the shattered door frame. As she watched her husband get in his truck, back out of the drive-way, and drive off Denise just dropped to her knees and began to cry uncontrollably.

Driving to the main highway Cedric's heart was still racing, eyes burning with anger, and hating his life at the moment. Swerving back and forth through traffic he began to calm down and realize what just happened, also what he did to his beautiful home and wife. Cedric immediately drove to his younger brother's house hoping he was home. Cedric's brother, Kareem Daniels, the baby boy of the two boys, always was more mature of the two and Cedric knew that. He needed his brother's guidance and help at this present time. Plus Kareem was a bachelor, their business would only be their business and no worries of a girlfriend or another wife jumping down his throat, asking "what's his problem." Cedric knew he had to find someone to repair the front door to the house and fast cause it's almost quitting time and the sun is going down fast in the Big Easy. When Cedric pulled up in Kareem's driveway, his younger brother of only 4 years was sitting on his porch conversing with two very beautiful young women. As he jumped out the truck all you could hear is, "What's happening Big Dawg?", shouted Kareem as he stepped off the porch. Giving one another dap, a tight hug, and a kiss on the cheek as they always have since they were teenagers. Cedric whispered in Kareem's ear, "We really need to talk, like right now. Alone." Looking at his older brother eye to eye with so much concern and seeing so much hurt in his eyes all Kareem did was turn to the young women and stated, "Say baby girl I'll holla at you two later alright." Cedric walked in the house, sat on the couch, and buried his face in his hands. With all the sentiment in the world Kareem sat next to his big brother and simply asked, "Ced what's the matter? What happened, man?" "I fucked up I really fucked up Reem", replied Cedric. While Cedric started his story, Kareem went and got two beers, sat down, and listened without any interruptions. Cedric begged, "Dude I gotta find a

19

contractor or a carpenter who can fix the door now." Kareem picked up his cell phone, scrolled through the address book, and began dialing.

"Hey Curtis, what's happening man? I need a real big favor, can you help me out? My brother needs a new door on his house like two hours ago, can you do it?", stated Kareem on the cell. "Money is not an issue", whispered Cedric. Kareem just nodded and brushed his brother's response off as he listened to the other person on the other end of the phone. "Damn that much. Well my brother said money's not an issue so how fast can you get over there", responded Kareem. Kareem said "Ok" and hung up the phone. Kareem's friend Curtis was a carpenter and was happy to help his friend's brother out but for a small fee of two thousand dollars, for the door, labor, and the short notice. Kareem sat down and explained the whole situation to Cedric and he agreed without hesitation. Curtis remembered where Cedric's house was because of all the cook outs and get-togethers that were held at the house. So all he had to go get was the door.

Cedric and Kareem chilled in the living room while waiting on Curtis' call. "Man what's taking so long? He should be finish by now or at least close to it." Cedric blurted aloud. Kareem calmly replied, "Ced it's only been a couple of hours. He had to go and get the door, measure it, and I don't know a whole bunch of other shit. Calm down and finish your beer. Curtis will call when he's done." Kareem couldn't help and wonder if Denise's allegations were true or not so he did what he always do. When you don't know the exact truth you go to the source and find it. Kareem was a psych major at Grambling University and he knew how to get the truth out of his brother without him even realizing what's going on. Kareem got up and went to his custom made bar in the corner of the living room, ducked down, and announced, "Ok now it's time for something a little stronger." Cedric could hear ice colliding together in what he could only imagine was two drinking glasses. Kareem knowing how much his brother favors Tequila more than any other liquor grabbed the clear round corked bottle of Patron, some limes, and two glasses filled with ice and placed it in front of Cedric on the coffee table. "I ain't trying to get ya drunk, I can see you had a rough day, and you need to relax", stated Kareem as he reclined back into his chair. Cedric couldn't do anything but shake his head yes and pull the cork out of the bottle and commence to pouring them both a drink. "We always had our arguments but never this bad, Reem. I mean if you would have seen her face and saw how she looked at me. She don't ever wanna see me again", stated Cedric as he sipped on his drink. Then with a confused look on his face Cedric finished, "Plus she really thinks that me and Sherell got something going on." Kareem thinking to his self that there's no better time than the present simply replied, "Well do you?" "No man, not you too", responded Cedric, then finished with, "For the record to clear it all up for you. Sherell and I have never had any kind of sexual contact in any way, period. The girl is a really good friend,

22

someone I could talk to about anything, and that's it. True she does like me a little more than I do her but she knows how far that can only go. Yes she is a very attractive woman but I love my wife. I really do love my wife with all my heart." Kareem looked at his brother and couldn't do anything but believe him. "Alright Big Dawg, I believe you I really do", replied Kareem. The two guys got up from the couch, went outside, and sat on the porch for some fresh air. "This a hell of a way to start a vacation, man", stated Cedric. That's when Kareem realized his brother was about to go on his month long vacation from his job. "Well this gives you and Denise a lot of time together to work your shit out. If I remember right you two going on a cruise somewhere right" , replied Kareem. That's when Cedric thought about all the fun him and his wife was supposed to have in Aruba. He saved up, penny pinched, and even denied himself lunch for about two months so they would be able to go on this two week cruise. Some people told him that 6 dollars a day wouldn't really make a difference, but if you add those 6 dollars to 60 days, he saved up 360 dollars. He looks at it now as a waste of time and effort. Denise even started exercising stating she felt she was getting a little thick around the middle and she wanted to show off her new designer two piece. They both were so ready for this little bit of 'peace and relaxation'. Kareem seeing the pain in his big brother's eyes tried to make him laugh or at least perk up a little blurted out, "Man you two were supposed to make me a niece or nephew, you know your mamma waiting on a grandchild from you.""Alonna and Shalay gave her eight that should be enough", replied Cedric smiling. Alonna and Shalay Daniels are the boys' twin sisters, Alonna being the older twin while Shalay the younger combined had 8 kids. Alonna with 2 boys and 1 girl, Devin the oldest is 18, Semaj the middle child is 14, and Dashanae the baby girl is 10. Alonna had her first child at the tender age of 14 while Shalay with 3 girls and 2 boys, Khori her oldest boy is 17, Ronnisha the oldest girl is 13, Zachariah is 9, Shantee is 5, and the baby girl Lenelle is 18 months had her first right behind her sister at the age of 15. "What have them two been up to anyways. I hadn't talked to them in a couple of days", asked Cedric. Kareem is a proud owner of two barber shop/salons and he loves his nieces and nephews. With Kareem looking down the street as if he were looking for his sisters replied, "Well Alonna was supposed to bring the boys over by the shop and I was gonna get one of the barbers to line them up. Shalay brought the girls last weekend to get their hair braided. That was utter chaos."

"Chaos? What happened when the girls got to the salon?", asked Cedric with a baffled look. Kareem put his head down and started laughing aloud to himself, "Where should I start? First of all Shalay looked like she had those kids hyped on candy 'cause they ran in the shop like they was at a track meet. Ronnisha wanted her braids to match her school colors." Cedric asked, "Ain't her school colors black and gold?" Kareem quickly responded, "Exactly, but that's not it. Dashanae and Shantee wanted pink braids." Cedric immediately started laughing out loud. "That shit's not funny. I got a rep to keep up", replied

Kareem. Cedric still laughing asked, "So what did you have the stylist do to their hair?" Shaking his head Kareem replied, "I had them put black hair with gold tips in Ronnisha's hair and black hair with pink streaks in Dashanae and Shantee's hair. They wasn't walking out of my shop looking like clowns. Like I said I got a rep. My baby Lenelle was the best behaved one." "She probably was sleeping half the time anyways, and you want me to have a kid. I know I was bad and my kid would probably be worst than me", replied Cedric. Before Kareem could respond to what Cedric had said the phone started ringing. Kareem picked up the phone, "Hello. Yeah what's up Curt? That's good, it looks alright? Good good, well pass over by the crib and I'll have your money waiting for you."It was Curtis on the phone letting Kareem know that he was finish and the old door was disposed of but Curtis then told Kareem some news that was really unsettling. When Curtis got to Cedric's house the police was already there talking to a very upset Denise sitting in the back of an ambulance. The N.O.P.D. officer asked Curtis did he know of Cedric's whereabouts but Curtis reply was that he was called by Denise's brother-in-law Kareem to come and fix the door. The police got Kareem's address and Curtis advised that Cedric should leave the area as soon as possible and try to call his wife to resolve the matter. "Damn she called the police on my ass", muttered Cedric as he wrote out the two thousand dollar check for Curtis. Kareem just replied, "Dude don't worry bout it. Just get over there, you and your wife talk, and explain to the cops it was a miss understanding and it won't ever happen again." Cedric got into his truck and before closing the door looked his brother square in the face and simply stated, "Thanks for everything, from the help all the way down to the good laughs, I love you Reem." "Right back at cha, big dawg. Now enough of that mushy shit, go get your wife some flowers, and commence to kissing a whole lotta ass", replied Kareem.

Cedric drove up the street and was taking his little brother's advice, he stopped at a near by florist and bought 3 dozen yellow roses. As he exited the flower shop all he could see was police lights behind his truck. Cedric's heart began beating nervously, his hands shaking, and his eyes as wide as silver dollars. When he got close to the police car he noticed that the officer was writing a traffic violation for the vehicle in front of him. The officer turned and looked at Cedric, "I'll be out your way in a minute sir." Cedric removed his

heart out his ass and let out a nervous smile, waved at the cop, and jumped into his truck. Thinking he's on 'America's Most Wanted' now for battery or assault, Cedric ducked down into the SUV hoping the policeman doesn't recognize him, waited 'til the cop moved the patrol car, drove off with seat belt on, and both hands on the steering wheel. He got on the Interstate and attempted to get home as quick as possible. Bobbing and weaving thru traffic as if all the other cars were parked on the I-10. Cedric drove up to his exit and down the exit ramp. As he approached the intersection Cedric did the one thing that all driving instructors and accident experts said never to do. He got distracted from keeping his eyes on the road and looked down at the roses he had just bought his wife. Thinking of how much he really does love her and how sorry he is for the events that lead up to this moment. When Cedric looked up and thru his driver side window his life flashed before his eyes. All he could really see was the grill of an eighteen-wheeler inches from his truck; he had ran the red light.

Boom!!! The vehicles collided and the black SUV flipped continuously five to six times while the big rig slowly came to a halt. Finally with wheels pointing straight up to the sky the wreckage that resembled a large black vehicle stopped tumbling and rested in a six foot deep canal. On-lookers jumped out of their cars and trucks to see if they could be of any assistants to either victims of the horrific accident they just witness. Half ran to the canal while the other half ran to the trucker stumbling out of his rig. Supporting the trucker up on his spaghetti legs to the sidewalk, several people asking him is he ok, all the trucker kept asking was the person in the SUV ok. Six or seven people stood at the top of the canal recording the event and calling for help on their cell phones while three Samaritans dove into a canal littered with yellow rose petals. One lady with fear that someone won't make it said, "It sounded like a bomb going off when they hit. It'll be a surprise if they're still alive after all that." The three men in the canal tugged and pulled at the battered doors of the truck. One of the guys kicked out the windshield and grabbed hold of Cedric's legs. The other two finally helped pull him out and to the grassy side where a few amazed spectators stood. Some were sickened by Cedric's lifeless, battered, and bruised body as the sound of an oncoming ambulance approached. As one woman crying as if it were her own child laying in the grass knelt down beside Cedric's head, holding it still, kept reassuring his motionless body, "Here they come, baby. Here they come."

Two ambulances arrived with tires screeching to a halt and the paramedics jumped out the vehicles. They split up, one set making assessments of the recovering truck driver and the others looking over Cedric's injuries. With the paramedic calling for the gurney out the back of the ambulance, he assured the upset woman still kneeling down next to Cedric that he's going to be ok. As the police arrived for their investigation of the accident, the medical team carefully eased Cedric onto the gurney and strapped him down to keep from

further injuries. "He has a very weak pulse and breathing is irregular, get him on some oxygen stat", stated one of the paramedics as he felt Cedric's wrist, noticed a police officer trying to get his attention. "Yeah, can I help you", said the rushing medic. The policeman replied, "I see you're real busy but do you have any idea what happened here?" "No not really but those people over there may know something. Those 3 guys were the ones who pulled him out of the wreckage", answered the medic. The officer went to the 3, exhausted soaking wet, gentlemen wrapped in blankets and greeted them as if they were living heroes, "Hey guys you did a great job in saving that guy's life." One of the men, an older Caucasian male, simply responded, "We did what we hope anyone would do for us." While nodding his head in agreement wishing the world had more people like them the police officer had some questions for the men. Before the officer began questioning the witnesses he ran over to the medics who were loading Cedric into the back of the ambulance to ask them a final question, "What hospital are you bringing him and the trucker to?" "I guess University your partner had to talk the trucker into going get checked out at least", replied one medic as he buckled himself in. The policeman then walked back over to the three 'heroes', as the two ambulances sped off with sirens blaring, for a little enlightenment on the devastating accident, with pad and pen in hand the law man, "Well did any of you see what happened here?" An African-American male in his early 20's stood up and started the disastrous story off, "Well I was directly behind the black suburban on the exit ramp. He just ran the light. It wasn't like he was trying to beat the light cause it had changed to red before we got to the bottom of the ramp. He just cruised dead across the light and that's when the eighteen-wheeler came."

The other two men gave their statements coinciding with the first gentleman's. The officer took down their names, information, and thanked them again for their heroism. The two partners met up at their squad car and compared information as they sat down in the patrol vehicle. The crowd started to clear as one tow truck driver tried to figure out how he was going to get the upside down SUV out of the canal. The big rig tow truck driver had successfully hooked and raised his cargo and went over to assist his fellow tow truck companion out with his ordeal.

CHAPTER 2

        Not knowing of the plethora of events that just occurred

involving her husband, Denise sat in her living room still highly

upset over his outrage earlier this evening. The phone started

ringing, she automatically assumed it was Cedric calling to

apologize and beg for her forgiveness. Part of her was pleased that

he made the first move to fix what she felt was all his fault while

the other half just wanted to, teach him a lesson and ignore the

call, let the phone ring off the hook 'til the answering service

intercepts. Aggravated at the sound of the ringing phone Denise

answers the phone, "Hello, who is it?" It was Alonna on the other

end just calling to see how her brother and only sister-in-law were

doing. "Dang, how you doing girl? I was just calling you two to

see what's been up", replied Alonna, who had no idea of the

events that has past. Denise angrily responded, "Well you need to

make room for your brother cause he won't be sleeping

here tonight." "What are you talking about", asked Alonna. "That nigger clicked out on me and kicked my damn door in. He took it clean off the hinges, with his crazy ass. I'm fed up and I can't deal with his shit anymore", answered a flared up Denise. Alonna trying not to get in the middle of the bickering simply replied, "Ok, well let me call him on his cell to see where he's at." "You won't get him on his cell. His bitch got his damn cell", responded Denise. Alonna confused even more now asked, "Who?" Denise answering with the coldest of heart, "That bitch Sherell got his cell phone." Alonna, trying not to add to the conflict and get into an argument with her sister-in-law, she simply got off the phone with her but before hanging up Denise finished, "and I called the police on that bitch too so if you hear from him let him know that." Alonna has known Sherell almost as long as Cedric has and knew how much her brother loved his wife but also how much he cared for Sherell. In fact, the two women are indeed real close friends plus Sherell is the Godmother of Alonna's only girl Dashanae who she loves dearly because she has no girls only a 13 year old boy by the name of Lamaj. Alonna figured her younger brother Kareem may know where Cedric may be if he's not already at his house hiding out. Before she called Kareem she had to call and gossip with her twin Shalay who enjoys what she calls some 'juicy gossip'. Shalay looks at her caller-id and answers the phone, "What Alonna? What did Devin do this time?" figuring her nephew is in trouble again. "Nope not my baby he's been good", replied Alonna. She continued, "Bitch, guess what happened with Ced and Denise earlier today?" With an excited voice Shalay asked, "What girl? What?" "Them two got into a heated argument and Ced kicked the door in on her ass. Then she called the police on him but he left before they got there", answered Alonna. "That 'stankin' bitch called the police on him", asked Shalay. Shalay never really cared for Denise because she feels Denise looks down on her because Shalay has five kids and is not married to any of the men who fathered the children. "Ok he did kick the door in on the girl", responded Alonna. Thinking just like her sister Shalay wanted to hear the story from her brother's mouth so she suggested in calling Kareem. Alonna clicked over to call their little brother on three-way to hear the whole story. Shalay then said as the phone was ringing, "And if the bitch was telling a lie on my brother, I swear I'm gonna go over there and whip her ass. You know I don't like that stuck up bitch anyways." Hearing part of the conversation, as he entertained the two beautiful young women who returned back to his house for what you can only call a 'night cap', Kareem answers the phone, "Who's a stuck up bitch?" Alonna responds, "Nobody, where is Ced cause I know he's there." "I guess you heard the news about Ced and Denise", asked Kareem. Kareem then let his two sisters know that Cedric had left the house over two and a half hours ago and should be home by now trying to save his marriage. "He's not home cause I just recently got off the phone with Denise before I called you", replied Alonna.

It was almost midnight and Denise was just getting out of the shower when she heard the phone ringing. Running through the bedroom dripping wet and trying to put on her terrycloth robe she answers the phone out of breath, "Hello!" A very professional sounding gentleman on the other end of the line with a foreign accent responds, "Hello, I'm sorry for calling this late but do you know a gentleman by the name of Cedric Daniels, African-American male, age 31, and last known address 5236 Revel Street Metairie, Louisiana?" Denise thinking it's the police and they're calling to let her know that they have Cedric in custody, "Yeah, that's my husband and?" "Well, Mrs. Daniels, your husband has been in an extremely bad accident and he's at University Hospital. The ER doctors are still working on him but they do have him somewhat stable. As soon as you can, you can come up here because the doctors may have some questions to ask you plus they would be better qualified to answer any questions you may have for them." Denise dropped the phone in disbelief, hoping she was dreaming and soon she'll be waking up from this nightmare of a day but all she could hear was the gentleman's voice coming out of the phone that was laying on the floor. In a daze she quickly said, "I'll be there as soon as I can." She threw on some clothes, grabbed her purse with I.D., and headed for the door. In a hysterical panic she searched for her car keys but realized her car wasn't outside and dropped to the floor into a cry that can't be described any other way but being obviously a painful breakdown. She felt she had no way to get to her extremely injured husband. Not even thinking of calling Cedric's family she called her sister Yolanda to see if she could come and pick her up to bring her to the hospital. Denise and Yolanda are literally one another's best friend since birth, Yolanda being the oldest at 30 and Denise being 27 looks to her big sister for guidance a lot and this time needing her more than ever. Denise big sister with no hesitation let her know that she's on her way to come and get her. Yolanda Patton, a strong single independent principal for a junior high school, has a heart of gold when it comes to her sister but can be a tad bit crude and unmoving with others. Never really caring for her brother-in-law's family, she felt they were in her words "Ghetto-fabulous", with what she saw as a womanizing thuggish younger brother, and twin sisters who look for love in all the wrong places and all they have to show for it are some 'bad ass kids'. Yolanda felt that Cedric was the only descent sibling out the bunch who at least had something going for him. As she told Denise several times, "How do they feel they have accomplished career jobs with Alonna being a bank teller, Shalay a hotel manager, and Kareem runs a barber shop, none of them having a degree in anything." Little does Yolanda know, Alonna is a Financial Analyst for Bank of America, Shalay is the General Manager and Program Director of the Airport Hilton by Armstrong International Airport, and Kareem doesn't only have a degree in Psychology and run his two barber shops/salons but he owns them, plus he's looking to get another shop built from the ground up. Denise see headlights shine through her front window and knows it's her loving sister Yolanda. She darts outside and the women meet one another on the porch. "C'mon let's go, let's go", Denise said frantically as she locked the door to the house. "What happened, baby", asked Yolanda as she backed out of the driveway. Denise, crying to no end, replies, "All I know is that he got in a really bad accident and the doctors are still working on him." Yolanda didn't need to know anything else, she sped to the hospital as fast as her car could go.

It was one o'clock Saturday morning and Delores Daniels, the mother of Alonna, Shalay, Cedric, and Kareem Daniels, woke up out of a sound sleep with unease in her bones, something just didn't feel right. This young 61 year old widow and mother felt she needed to check on each of her children, something she did on a regular basis but this time she really felt something was amiss. She started with her baby boy Kareem and found him still entertaining at his house, Alonna and Shalay bought answered their phones with sleep in their voices, but when she called Cedric's home there was no answer. This didn't rest easy with Delores so then she thought to call his cell phone, maybe he and his wife went out to a club. She flips through her little address book, finds her oldest boy's cell number and begins dialing with severe anxiety in her stomach. The phone rings about three times when the most appealing female voice comes across, "Hello."

"Hey, Denise", responds Delores with a bit of question in her voice as if she had dialed the wrong number. Recognizing the elderly woman's voice, "No Mrs. Delores this is Sherell, Sherell White, Cedric dropped his cell at work and I didn't have a chance to bring it to his house. Is everything ok?" Delores surprised by this had no other choice but to ask Sherell, "Yeah, everything's alright and I'm so sorry to bother you but have you heard from Cedric or Denise today?" Starting to become a little concerned for the, home alone, up in age woman Sherell asks if she could be of any assistance plus lets Delores know that the last time she spoke to any of them was when she called Denise to let her know of Cedric's cell. "Well baby I just don't feel right, you know maybe it's a mother's intuition, but I called Ced's house and no one answered", replies Delores as worry starts to set in. Sherell assures the worrying mother that she's going to call Alonna and see if she knows where Cedric and Denise are. "Thank you, baby, thank you", replied Delores as she hangs up the phone. The phone rings again at Alonna's house and this time she's obviously agitated after being waken up by her mother the first time answers the phone with tension in her voice this time, "Hello." Sherell hearing the roughness in Alonna's voice apologized for waking her up. She then explained the reason for the late call and that Alonna's mother mistakenly called her looking for Cedric and Denise. Alonna then asked why they didn't just call Denise's cell phone, she may know where he is. Sherell then suggested that she'll call Denise and Alonna quickly stopped her, "Nah, I'll call her and see if she knows where Ced is." Sherell noticed how Alonna stated that and asked, "Why you say it like that?" Alonna tried to brush it off by replying, "Nothing girl, nothing. It's just that Denise is trippin' right now cause her and Ced got into an argument and you have his cell phone." "What are you talking about, I called her and told Denise that Ced dropped his cell at work", replies Sherell clearly upset now. Sherell then further went on in saying, "Denise has nothing to worry about when it comes down to Ced and I. Yes I do really care for Ced but I love him as a friend and that's it. Besides Denise is Cedric's everything and that's something I envy and cherish. I could never get in between that, shit to be honest it's immoral and down right wrong. I love him too much to do that to him." "Ok girl, ok calm down you made your point it's all good with me", responded Alonna with a smile on her face, thinking to herself that Denise should have heard that. Alonna then told Sherell to hold on while she clicks over and calls Denise's cell. The phone rings and rings 'til the answering service comes on and Alonna hangs up and calls right back. Now getting worried like her mother Alonna patiently waits for an answer while making the comment, "Ok she usually answers her phone and if she's home she turns the phone off and the answering service picks up automatically, why no answer?" Finally the ringing stops and a woman answer, "Yes hello", it was Yolanda on the other end. "Denise, everything ok over there", asked Alonna. Yolanda replies, "This is her sister, she can't talk right now but I can take a message." Alonna knew who it was and asked Yolanda if Denise and Cedric were together but the news

Yolanda gave her disturbed both of the women on the phone, "Well there's been an accident and Cedric's in the hospital. Denise is talking to the doctors right now and I don't know what's going on, we just got here about forty-five minutes ago." Sherell mumbles, "Oh my God."

"Why didn't anybody call us", asked Alonna. "Well I was trying to get Denise to her husband first", comments Yolanda. "Husband or not, he's still my brother. What hospital is he in", replied Alonna. Yolanda tells Alonna that they are at University Hospital in the Intensive Care Unit of the ER and that they're waiting on news from the doctor in charge of Cedric's treatment. Alonna immediately got off the phone with Yolanda and started calling her siblings to tell them the bad news. "Do you want me to call your mother and tell her while y'all go to the hospital", asked Sherell. "Please, cause I don't think I could handle her right now", said Alonna. Sherell pleads with Alonna to let her know of Cedric's condition when she gets

45

some more info and also if she needs anything don't hesitate to ask. Alonna agrees and heads out to meet her brother and sister at the hospital while Sherell sits worrying at home. Sherell calls Delores to tell her the bad news of her oldest boy being in the hospital. She tries to comfort the nerve-racked mother by letting her know that everything's going to be ok. She then volunteered her services by offering to come over for more support if needed. Delores gladly welcomes the visit with open arms, "Please baby cause I can't be over here by myself wondering what's going on down there with them. If you don't mind, I really don't wanna put you out your way", pleads the frantic mother. "Well let me let Lamaj know that I'll be leaving and to keep the door locked, ok", replied Sherell. "No, please bring my handsome little man. He always seems to brighten up my day when he's here and he won't be bored cause Semaj left his little video games here hooked to the TV", implores Delores. Sherell agreed and she and Lamaj headed out to Delores'house. Delores like everyone else except for Denise really liked Sherell, she even looked at her as a daughter figure. With Alonna and Sherell becoming real close friends and Sherell being Dashanae's Godmother just put the icing on the cake for the love that Delores has for who she calls a "Precious Angel". Sitting nervously in her rocking chair Delores did the one thing that always seems to calm her down, she went to the kitchen and began cooking her famous breakfast. She turned on all four burners and had a pot or skillet for each one, the first one was for pancakes, the second for eggs, the third was for bacon, sausage, thin-cut pork chops, and the fourth was some creamy but thick and buttery grits.

Delores laid out all the food as if the President of the United States were coming over for breakfast. After preparing this wonderful first meal of the day she started washing up all the dishes left over. As she submerged her hands into the bubble filled kitchen sink a knock came at the door. "I'm coming", alerted Delores. Opening the door to a half sleep 13 year old Lamaj, "Hey Nanna, moms parking the car, she's coming." Delores just grabbed him in her arms and held on so tight she cut off his breathing. Sherell walked in on the tight embrace and just let out a sincerely emotional sigh of appreciation, that her son would show this woman not his grandmother love and respect as if she were. "Hey Mrs. Dee, how you doing", stated Sherell with worry in her eyes. Delores just reached over and grabbed hold of Sherell and held on as if she was holding on for dear life. The hug answered all of Sherell's questions, but she needed the hug also as much as Delores did. The smell of all the food got Lamaj's attention and he ran straight for the table stating as he walked away, "Nanna this food for me?" "Yeah baby, let me dish it up for you. Sit down Sherell I'll dish yours up too", replied Delores. Sherell let Delores know she didn't have that to do, but Delores being a mother and grandmother first just brushed her comments off. Delores dished up two big plates of food for the two early morning visitors and Lamaj had an appetite of ten teenagers.

Kareem and the twins walked through the automatic opening emergency doors to find Denise and her sister sitting patiently next to the nurses' station. Alonna walked up to Yolanda and simple asked, "Where is he?" Alonna and Shalay still angered that Denise did not call them to inform them of their brother's accident ignored the reply and went straight to an unsuspecting nurse walking from behind the nurses station. Kareem just sat down next to Denise and buried his head in his hands in utter disbelief that his older brother was in the hospital in God knows what condition. "Excuse me, I don't mean to bother you, but my brother is back there. His name is Cedric Daniels, he was in a car accident, and I was just wondering what's going on with him", begged Shalay. The nurse replied, "I'm going back there now to bring the doctor these charts and I'll let him know you all are up here waiting ok. He should be up here shortly." Alonna thanked the nurse for her cooperation and began pacing back and forth down the aisle worrying the worse. She figured if she expects the worse then the doctor would come through the doors with good news. "I need a cigarette", stated Yolanda as she stood up and walked to the exit doors with Denise following like a little puppy. Cedric's siblings stared in astonishment as they watched their brother's wife walk out the door instead of waiting for any news of her husband's condition. "And you wonder why I don't like the bitch", stated Shalay as she rested her head on her little brother's shoulder. "Well baby, I guess I'll be going ok. Your in-laws are here now, you could sit and wait with them", indicated Yolanda as she pulled out her car keys from her purse. "No, you're my only family here and I don't think I could do this by myself. Please Yolanda don't leave", pleaded Denise.

Yolanda then turned to Denise and let her know that when she married Cedric, that his family became her family so she's not alone. Denise holding onto her big sister's hand begged that she stay and Yolanda complied. As Yolanda stood on the ramp of the emergency driveway, she blew smoke out of her nose like a Brahma bull. That's when Kareem came rushing through the sliding doors to let them know that the doctor came with some disturbing news. Denise and Yolanda walked in seeing Shalay and Alonna holding one another crying intensely. "What's wrong, what's wrong", cried Denise. "Hi Mrs. Daniels, my name is Dr. Jerome Walters, I'm the doctor in charge of your husband's care", acknowledged Walters. Dr. Walters sat Denise down and gave her the news that he just gave to his siblings. Dr. Walters then stated with great remorse, "What I'd like to let you know first is that Cedric is stable but he is on a respirator. He did have some substantial injuries, such as broken collar bones, a dislocated shoulder, two broken ribs, a broken leg, and a skull fracture. We lost him twice but he's a strong willed individual. The only thing is that with those two times that his heart stopped pumping, oxygen wasn't flowing through his bruised brain and with that entire trauma he fell into a coma." Denise couldn't believe the words that were coming out of Dr. Walters' mouth but she couldn't take her eyes off his face. She felt if she turned and looked toward Kareem and the twins they would look at her with so much animosity, feeling it was her fault that their brother was in the condition he was in. Dr. Walters then stated, "Now there's one good thing about Cedric being in this coma." Alonna wiping her face with a tissue asked, "What could be good about a coma?" Dr. Walters replied, "Well with him being in a coma he won't have to go through all the pain of his injuries and the surgery of us resetting his leg back in place. Now the down fall of the coma is that we really don't know when he would come out of the coma and also he may have some serious brain damage." Kareem asked, "Brain damage! What brain damage?" Dr. Walters replied, "Well there's a strong possibility that he won't be totally himself. Being that his brain suffered hypoxia, which is another word for a shortage of oxygen, he might come out of his coma in a vegetative state. Now I'm not saying this is all a definite but worse case scenario that's all. I'm just warning you in advance of the possibilities and not to get your hopes up high of a full recovery. We're going to take this one day at a time." Kareem being the man of the distraught family grabbed hold of Dr. Walters hand and thanked him for his help and service, so did Yolanda. "Can I see my brother, please", asked Shalay. Dr. Walters told them that they could visit with him for a little while but also let them know that all the bandages and tubing would be a little disturbing to an unwary viewer. He then walked the family to the back of the intensive care unit and before opening the door to the room he stated; "Now I know some people say that comatose patients can't hear you when you speak to them but I encourage it. He's not going to respond but who knows it may help him in the process." Dr. Walters opened the door and let the group walk into what you would call hell. A disturbing image of Cedric laying in a hospital bed with numerous tubes exiting from under the sheet, his head wrapped up, and various parts of his body covered in bandages or a cast. Kareem just stood in the doorway as if he was scared to get any closer. The tears flowed even heavier out of Alonna and Shalay's eyes as they watched their brother knocking on the door of death. Yolanda couldn't make it to the bed as she fell into a chair close to the doorway where Kareem still stood. Denise calmly walked up to her husband's bed and slid her hand under his wishing he would grab hold of it. She turned to Dr. Walters looking at him with those big brown eyes and simple said in an asking way, "He's not grasping to my hand?" "Well baby he doesn't know you're here, I'm sorry", replied Dr. Walters. As she was crying Alonna stated, "Oh my God, I need to call mommy and Sherell to let them know what's going on. Kareem could you do it cause I really don't think I could." Kareem agreed and walked out toward the exit still in a state of bewilderment over his brother's outcome of today's events.

As he walked to the double sliding doors he could hear quarreling in the room but he figured his sisters are just letting out their hurt that they feel for their brother's pain. With no idea of what an event has past, Delores and Sherell with Lamaj sat and enjoyed one another company laughing at Lamaj as he tries to get the high score on the video game. The sun began to peak through the antique designed curtains of the living room when the phone rang. Delores jumped out her seat to get the phone and answered quickly, "Yes, hello…Yeah she's here why…No, tell me I need to know what's going on? Kareem, tell me." She dropped the phone to her chest, turned to Sherell, and quietly said, "Kareem wants to talk to you." Sherell wondering why, had a perplexed look on her face as she grabbed hold of the phone, "Hey Kareem, what's up?" Sherell sat quiet on the couch listening to every word that came out of Kareem's mouth wishing that she wasn't the one who had to bear this horrendous news to Delores. The news of her friend's faith cut through her like a hot knife would butter. Looking in Delores' worried eyes she already knew the outcome of what this information would do to the impatiently waiting mother of four. Sherell whispered into the phone, "Kareem I can't do this why didn't you tell her?" "Rell, c'mon I can't. I need you to do it please 'cause I got enough on my plate trying to keep Alonna, Shalay, and myself together with a little composure", replied Kareem. Still talking to Sherell, Kareem could hear the squabbling that he heard earlier got extremely loud and got his attention. He turned

to see his twin sisters being escorted by hospital police with

Denise and Yolanda following right behind them in the same

predicament. Kareem let Sherell know that he had to go

immediately, "What the hell happened now? Baby girl I gotta go

like right now. That composure just fell apart as we speak."

Sherell hung up the phone and turned to Delores, "Mama there's

been a problem." "Just tell me is he alive", asked the already

crying mother. "Yes, yes he is. It's just that he's banged up really

bad and in a coma", replied Sherell as tears began falling down

her face.

Kareem ran to his sisters' aid hoping everybody wasn't

going to jail, "What the hell happened here?" "They started

fighting back there in the ICU and we don't tolerate actions like

that", replied an angered gentleman with a badge on his chest

stating "University Hospital Police". Kareem told the frustrated

policeman that he would take over the situation and insured it won't happen again. Frustrated himself, Kareem asked what's the reason for the altercation and also indicated no matter what the reason it's not the time or place for it. Alonna told him what started the whole brawl in the beginning, "She got mad 'cause Rell is over by mama waiting to see how Ced is doing. Denise whatever you did to get'em you gotta do to keep'em and evidently you ain't doing it cause you scared somebody else is gonna take your man." "Somebody needs to let the bitch know that everything doesn't revolve around her", replied Shalay. Answering Shalay's comment, "I don't give a damn about her, all I'm saying is why she has to be told what's going on in my life like that's her husband and not mine. If I want her to know about him I'll tell her." Kareem stood in between the women to avoid any punches being thrown but let Denise know that Sherell has been part of their family as a real good friend for more than 13 years. Stating Cedric is like a brother to her and his welfare is of concern to her. Yolanda then replied, "Y'all know that girl been liking on Ced for who knows how long and you ignore it or better yet encourage it 'cause you don't like my sister in the first place."

Shalay jumped in, "Yolanda for one you are not even part of this family. The only reason you're here is because your sister called you for a ride. When she married Ced, she married into this family and we love her as if she were our own sister. Like I said you are not part of this family so keep your mouth shut or I can keep it shut for you." Kareem let everyone know that the argument is over and done with, and then he escorted Denise and Yolanda to Yolanda's car. "Go home and try to get a little rest, ok. I'll call you later to check on you, alright Dee. Yolanda, thank you for coming", stated Kareem as he shut the car door. He then turned to his sisters to walk them to their cars stating as he walked, "Ok, I know you two don't really care for the girl, to tell you the truth I don't feel for the female my damn self but Ced loves that girl dearly. So with that being said you love her just like him right now. I don't wanna hear anymore arguments at all. If she tries to start one just ignore her ass and go on 'bout your business. Is that understood?" "All I'm saying is that she's more concerned about a female, Ced and our friend, than her husband's well being",

replied Shalay. Alonna just nodded in agreement with her sister as

she opened the door to her car, "Plus Sherell told me herself that

she could never interfere with Ced and Denise's marriage." "Well

let's put all that shit in the past and leave it at that, 'cause Ced

needs us more than ever and being a family is one of them",

specified Kareem as he turned to get in his car. The twins drove

off as Kareem sat in his car and watched them disappear down the

street. Alone in the car all of his emotions came rushing to

Kareem at once, trying to hold on, he just broke down from seeing

his brother the way he was. Kareem pulled himself together,

wiped the tears from his face and figured his mother needs him so

he picked up his cell phone to call her. To his surprise the cell

phone started ringing, it was Alonna calling letting him know that

she and Shalay were going by their mother's house, "I was just

wondering if you wanted to pass over by mama." Kareem started

his engine and answered, "I'll meet you two there."

The ride back to Cedric and Denise's house was quiet and just down right uneasy. Neither girls knew what to tell one another for neither one of them ever been in a situation as such. Yolanda slowly pulled into the driveway and put the car in park. "You want me to come in with you", she asked. Denise just shook her head yes and got out of the car as if her body was falling limp. Yolanda asked, "Denise, you alright baby?" "I'm just drained completely, I can't take it anymore", replied Denise. The women walked into the home and sat at the dinning room table. Denise then began talking about how she can't get through this ordeal alone and how this was supposed to have been a happy time. Yolanda somewhat feeling her pain tried to console her sister by letting her know that she has her to lean on. "You're gonna be alright. Ced will get out of that coma and he's gonna be fine", responded Yolanda to her sister's cry outs. Denise answered, "But what if he doesn't? Am I gonna have to raise this baby on my own? I can't do this by myself, I swear I can't." Yolanda grasps hold of her sister's hand and asked, "Are you serious, you're

60

pregnant?" "Yes, I was supposed to wait and let Cedric know on our vacation. It was suppose to be a surprise. I've known for a month and a half now", answered Denise. In all the drama and heartache of today's events the women had reason to hug for a sensational reason. Denise's pregnancy is now Yolanda's main priority and highest ranking event to her. Denise felt the same way but still had Cedric in the back of her mind wondering if he would be able to help raise the newborn. She started worrying if when Cedric does come out of his coma would he be in a total vegetative state, does that mean she would have to raise a baby and take care of a grown adult in dire need of medical attention at all times? Denise was torn in between wanting to be a wife or being a first time mother, "I can't take care of him and take care of a baby. What am I gonna do", she asked. Yolanda tried to calm her little sister's nerves by trying to assure her that everything's going to be fine but the entire time all the newly impregnated woman could think of was if her baby would have a good life. Denise felt if she has to look after her comatose husband what time would she have for her baby. She loved children and always wanted a lot of kids for her own. She and Cedric tried to get pregnant several times but gave up a long time ago figuring they would be the favorite aunt and uncle who spoils their nieces and nephews. When Denise found out she was pregnant she couldn't believe it and waited to tell anyone because she just wanted to make sure for herself. "C'mon I'm gonna stay here with you, ok", stated Yolanda. She walked Denise upstairs to her bedroom and laid her in the big lonesome king sized bed. Yolanda, still in shock of the news her baby sister just revealed to her, headed to the guess bedroom down the hall so she could get a little rest herself. "Please don't leave me in here", begged Denise. Yolanda submitted and sat at the head of the bed as Denise just rests her head in her big sister's lap and began to fall asleep.

Lamaj seen his pretend aunts and uncle walking up to their mother's house and couldn't resist running outside to them, "Uncle Reem, y'all here", screamed Lamaj as he bear hugged

Shalay. The twins and Kareem spirits lifted when they seen the excited teenager greet them at the door but they knew their mother was inside panic-stricken over the fact that her oldest boy is in the hospital in a coma. "Mama told Nanna what happened. She's inside in her room", continued Lamaj as he walked in holding Alonna's hand. They all walked in to Sherell sitting on the couch, eyes swollen from all the crying and her nose still running, trying to hold herself together. Alonna and Sherell just latched on to one another in a tight embrace while Kareem headed straight to his mother's room to comfort her. Shalay tried to ease her own mind by talking to Lamaj, "So what have you been doing Mr. Man?" Kareem walked upstairs to his mother's room to her kneeling at the side of an immaculately put together bed. Seeing his mother in deep prayer made him feel that it was the only thing that would help his only brother at this time. Without even looking at him Delores put out her hand for her baby boy to kneel down and pray with his mother. Delores went on, "Lord please watch over your child Cedric and please take his hand and pull him out of that dark hole he's in right now. Watch over this family for we need You more than ever Lord. Amen." As Delores opened her eyes from prayer she noticed Kareem was crying silently and she couldn't do anything but reassure her youngest boy with a mother's hug to let him know everything will be ok. Sherell and Alonna sat holding each other's hands as if they were petrified to let go. Sherell had finally stopped crying and wanted to know how Cedric was fairing at the hospital. Shalay asked Lamaj to go in the backyard for a minute so she, Alonna, and his mother had a talk, she didn't want to talk about Cedric's injuries and condition in front of the teenager. The twins told Sherell everything that Dr. Walters told them, all the way down to the possibility that he may have some brain damage. The women started crying once again but then Sherell replied, "Well he did say it may be a possibility not a definite fact. A coma is still somewhat a mystery to doctors 'cause they don't know when a person would come out of a coma or how they would be as far as their brain goes. There has been people who have been in a coma for 2 to 3 weeks and come out perfectly fine and ones who have been in a coma for 2 to 3 years and come out the same way." Sherell was confident that Cedric's recovery would come out all right and she gave the twins a strong sense of hope for their brother and family. As the girls sat in the living room confident that all will be fine, Kareem and Delores came downstairs to Shalay telling Sherell of the conflict that happened in the hospital. Sherell then stated, "I should call her and let her know that I'm just concerned about him and his family's wellbeing." "No, that wouldn't be a good idea right now", replied Kareem. "Well I'll just go to keep down the stress on her and y'all", responded Sherell. Alonna then let Sherell know that she's not causing any problems yet she's actually helping them cope with the circumstances, so Sherell stayed with the family and they gave one another comfort and support.

CHAPTER 3

Yolanda was in the kitchen preparing her baby sister a little something to eat while she slept. As she finished up and was getting ready to bring Denise a bowl of soup the telephone began ringing. The helpful big sister ran to answer the phone so not to let it wake Denise, "Yes, hello", answers Yolanda. It was Kareem on the other end checking on his sister-in-law, "Hey Yolanda this Reem, I was just calling to see how she was holding up." "She's sleeping right now but I guess she's alright", answers Yolanda. Thinking about the secret her sister just bestowed on her, Yolanda tries dearly not to spill the information to anyone, asked how Delores was at this rough time. Kareem assured her that his mother was either putting on a really good act or she was just being the rock that she is and holding their family together with faith. Yolanda, for the first time held a long conversation with Kareem, that wasn't an argument, and finally seen a side of him she never really knew. Kareem and Yolanda both were enjoying one another's conversation, keeping their minds occupied with good thoughts, kids, goals, and enjoying what they do for a living. "Well I'm gonna have to talk to you later, I gotta get to the shop and make sure my barbers aren't tearing the place up. It was really nice talking to you Yolanda", stated Kareem. "Ok then, I'll get Denise to call over there when she wakes up, call me later ok" replied Yolanda. After hanging the phone up she headed upstairs with the bowl, thinking to herself maybe Kareem isn't so bad after all. Not realizing or even thinking about the state of affairs that has just taking place with her sister's husband Yolanda begins to see the potential in Kareem and looks past the image; the shoulder length dreadlocks, designer named clothes, fancy jewelry, and luxury vehicle. She began to see a well intelligent and legally self-employed young African-American male with a lot going for himself but he just has a relaxed demeanor about himself. "What are you thinking about that got you all smiles", asked Denise as she woke to Yolanda sitting on the edge of the bed. She just replies, "Oh nothing", while reaching Denise her bowl of soup.

She then let Denise know that Kareem called to check on her and began giving him a little praise by stating, "He has a good head on his shoulders. Reem and I actually had a pretty descent conversation and I enjoyed it." Denise replied, "Don't get caught up, you know he's my age and you know how you feel about younger men." Yolanda thought to herself that age may not be an issue at this point.

Kareem stands outside his mother's home, smoking a cigarette, and staring into space as Sherell walks up behind him, "You know that stuff will kill you." "Yeah, but it's this or a stiff drink and I think it's just a little too early for some Whiskey shots", replied Kareem. Sherell trying to get Kareem to relax and smile responded, "Shit, it's never too early for some Crown on the rocks." He smiled but it was only done because he knew what she was trying to do. Kareem then headed for his car but not before letting his mother and sisters know he was leaving. He held Sherell by the hand as he walked to the car telling her how much he really appreciate her staying with them. They hugged one another as tight as they could and he kissed Sherell on her cheek stating, "Thank you so much. I really mean it. You just don't know how much you mean to this family. Shit you are family." Sherell just nodded in agreement with him but Kareem made her feel better instead of the other way around. She watched Kareem as he drove down the street and thought to herself that she has to see Cedric in person. Lamaj ran up to his mother stating, "Auntie Alonna told me to come get you because some man named Kevin is on Cedric's cell phone asking for him." Sherell knew it was going to be hard talking to Kevin, with Cedric and Kevin being real good friends, but he could be her excuse to go see Cedric for awhile. She walked in the house to Shalay smiling talking to Kevin on the phone, "…..yeah we're ok. Maybe we could see you soon besides when you come over to feed your face during Thanksgiving. Well here's Sherell, I'll talk to you later." Sherell got on the phone with Kevin to him asking when are they going to go see Cedric and why didn't she call him to let him know of

Cedric's accident. Kevin then told Sherell some shocking but marvelous news. He told her that he had called the hospital and used the clout that he was born with and had gotten Cedric a private room. Plus he had one of his father's partner search for two of the finest physicians who specialize in comatose patients. She was ecstatic and couldn't wait to tell the family. Sherell then told Kevin of Denise's displeasure of Cedric and her friendship, how she got into an argument with the twins, and the accusations that Cedric and her had an affair. Kevin assured Sherell that the friendship she and Cedric has is genuine and true. He further let her know that he wish he had someone like her in his life that would have his and his family back in good and bad times as she has. Further making Sherell feel better about being with the Daniels family during their time of need.

Alonna was sitting at the kitchen table with her mother trying to figure out what their next plan of action would be, "Mama, I know you want to see him but I really don't think it's a

70

good idea. I didn't want to walk in there but I needed to make sure he was alive. Plus after seeing him I wish I never walked through that doorway." Delores calmly responded, "If one of your kids were in the hospital wouldn't you want to see them, no matter what anyone tells you? It's a mother's love that has me wanting to see my son. Dead or alive, I need to see him face to face, and knowing he's alive has me wanting to see him even more. Being a mother you should understand that." Alonna just listened and understood totally but in the back of her mind was wondering if her mother could handle seeing her son in the condition that she just witnessed a few hours ago. She then let her mother know that after she checks on her children they all can go and see Cedric at the hospital. "I can't go see my brother like that again", answered Shalay as she walked in on her mother and sister's conversation. Shalay then commented, "Look, I'll go and check on the kids on my way home. So you and mama can just leave straight from here to the hospital." Alonna knew exactly how her twin felt being that she didn't want to go back this soon to see Cedric's battered, bruised, and limp body. The twins agreed and Delores went upstairs to get dressed so she can go and see her son. Sherell saw Delores rush up the stairs and began looking for the twins' whereabouts. Sherell couldn't wait to let the girls know of the good news Kevin had told her moments ago. She walked into the kitchen to Alonna and Shalay discussing if their mother would be able to handle seeing Cedric in the hospital. Shalay, feeling her mother is the strongest woman alive, said, "Mama will be able to handle it...remember she was there when daddy died." Alonna responded, "That was over twenty-five years ago too. She was a lot younger and different then. I'm just really thinking about if her heart can handle it." "What really happened to your father? If you don't mind me asking", asked Sherell. Before Alonna could get out a word Sherell then quickly declared, "You don't have to tell me if you don't want to, really." "No it's ok. I really don't mind talking about it", answered Alonna. She then went on, "It was August 31, 2005, two days after hurricane Katrina, and my dad was a sheriff for New Orleans. So you know he was out there during the riots and looting. My mom was at a hotel with us when our dad showed up to take us out of the city. She told us later the reason she didn't leave earlier was because if her whole family couldn't leave 'no one leaves…we never leave a man behind'. When my dad and the other sheriffs showed up to get their families out of the hotel, there were looters in there and some of them were trying to take the charter buses that were down stairs for the sheriffs' families. My dad wasn't having it at all, so he and his partner 'Uncle David' tried to hold the looters back with shotguns, by standing in front of the buses. From how the story was told to my mother, two of the guys jumped Uncle David and struggled with him with his shotgun. My dad was trying to help Uncle David and the shotgun went off and struck my dad point blank in his stomach. The other sheriffs were bringing all of us down right when it happened not even knowing what just took place. Uncle David was on his knees with his uniform shirt on my dad's stomach and my mom ran to be at my father's side. My dad looked up at my mom and immediately told her he was sorry and he loves her. She told Uncle David to take us on the bus and she sat there while havoc and carnage was going on around her with my father in her lap. They kissed and he died a few minutes later but before he did he told my mom he loves her so much and to kiss each one of his babies for him. My mama picked up my dad's shotgun and stood over his body in front of the charter bus to wait for the last family to get on. She said, '…he would have liked to finish his post no matter what.' I don't remember ever seeing my mother cry at all, I guess she was being strong for us. She never really wanted to come back to the city, said, '…it was dead to her, but I guess roots are roots.'"

Sherell stood listening attentively to every word, in shock all at the same time. Sherell herself had felt the lost of a parent, so she in a way knew how the twins felt about the subject. She lost both her parents at the same time tragically just like the twins but not the same way plus they still had their mother, Sherell didn't. "How old were you", she asked. "Well we were 8 years old at the time, Cedric was 6, and Kareem was just 2", answered Shalay.

Delores came down the stairs while the girls were still talking

with purse in hand, "Alright I'm ready." Sherell then remembered

why she walked in the kitchen looking for the twins, "Oh my God,

I almost forgot to tell y'all. When I was on the phone with Kevin,

he told me some great news. He pulled some strings and got

Cedric a private room and he also got two physicians who

specialize in comatose patients to work with Ced." Delores just

grabbed hold of Sherell and held on to her as tight as she could as

she whispered in her ear, "I Love you. You and Kevin are

blessings to this family, thank you baby, thank you." With tears in

her eyes Sherell just responded, "Well ok, let's go see him, Kevin

said he'll wait for us at the hospital because he really wants to see

Ced too." The ladies left with Lamaj running behind to keep up

with them. Sherell was more excited to see Cedric than his own

sisters as she rushed to back out of the driveway and lead the way.

"So we going see Cedric now, mama", asked Lamaj. Sherell

thinking to herself 'finally' replies, "Yeah baby, we just going for a little while and then we're gonna go home. I promise." Lamaj didn't mind going at all, he really liked Cedric and he was curious to see him also.

Yolanda was getting ready to leave when she heard Denise on the phone, "…now that is some wonderful news. I don't know what to do that would show my appreciation." Yolanda was inquiring what her sister was so happy about at this awful time in her life. She tried to snoop and listen from the other room as she gathered her belongings. After straining to be the nosy individual she naturally is Yolanda gave up and simply walked in the room and asked, "What's going on? What wonderful news?" Despite the worry still in her eyes Denise's face carried a smile as she turned to answer her troublesome sister, "I'll tell you in a minute." Yolanda put everything down she had gathered up and sat in the den waiting on her ecstatic little sister. "Thank you for calling me and I'll see you in a little while", stated Denise as she hung up the phone. She immediately ran searching for Yolanda to let her in on the great news she just got. Denise hurried into the den to her patiently waiting sister and told her the phone call was from a Dr. Johnston, Cedric's new specialist. Dr. Johnston called Denise to inform her that he and his colleagues would be in charge of Cedric's care from now on. Johnston gave out his credentials to Denise as if he were reading from his resume' itself. He also let her know that he's in route to the hospital to see Cedric and would love to meet her. "Well I guess we're heading back to the hospital then", asked Yolanda. Denise headed to the bedroom to get dressed and answered, "I'll go by myself, it's no problem. I know you probably tired by now." "Nah, I'm cool, just go get your stuff so we can roll out", replied Yolanda. Yolanda went outside to smoke a cigarette as she waited on Denise to get ready, wondered if Kareem and the twins knew of the new news that has come forward. When Denise came out the front door that same question that ran through Yolanda's head met her at the door. "Right now my main concern is me and my husband. When I meet with Dr. Johnston and he fulfills all my apprehensions about Cedric then

I'll call them", replied Denise as she closed the door to Yolanda's car.

Yolanda couldn't believe how heartless her little sister just sounded. Even though in her words she 'tolerates them only because of Cedric and Denise's marriage', Yolanda felt that family is family and they had the right to know. An argument was inevitable in her eyes as the two headed to the hospital, one with aspiration that her husband will be back with her and her unborn child soon enough, while the other braced herself for a family brawl. Yolanda knew the twins didn't really care for her as a person, being that she never showed them any love either, but she felt she had to get the news about Cedric to them somehow. She casually reached for her cell phone to search for Kareem's number. The phone rung a few times and Kareem answered, "Hey you. What's up? How's Denise holding up? I meant to call back to check on you two but a brother got a little busy at the shop. My contractor came over with the plans for my next salon and we been at it for a minute now. He wants marble counter-tops through out the whole shop and I keep telling him he is not paying for this, oak counter-tops would be fine. Listen to me just running at the mouth, telling you all my problems. What's up Londa?" Just listening to his voice Yolanda almost forgot why she had called him but then she didn't know how to go about talking to Kareem without little sister hearing the whole conversation. Right when she was about to blurt out what she needed to get off her chest Denise tapped her on her shoulder and pointed to a corner store, suggesting that Yolanda should pull over. "Hold on one second here, I need to make a quick stop", stated Yolanda. As Kareem patiently held the phone his call waiting beeped, "You hold on too, somebody's hitting me up." He answers his other line to hear his big sister Shalay on the other end, "Hey Reem, you not busy are you?" "No not really, what's up with cha", answers Kareem. Shalay replies, "Well we are headed back to the hospital to meet up with Cedric's friend Kevin. We were trying to get in touch with Denise so she could meet us there but she's not answering the house or her cell phone. I was wondering if you heard from her because we got some real good news for her and didn't want to leave her out of it." Shalay then went on to tell Kareem about what Kevin had done for their brother. Even though Denise and the twins never really see eye to eye the majority of the time they felt that she should be there, "….she is part of the family", and Shalay knew that Denise talks to Kareem more than they do. Kareem then remembered that he had Yolanda on hold and could relay the message through her, "…hold on one second." When he clicked over Yolanda had hung up the phone, so he told Shalay he'll get the news to Denise and got off the phone with her.

Yolanda began driving as slow as possible without Denise noticing, really just prolonging the already foreseen future. Denise was nibbling on a snack she had bought from the corner store when she noticed all the other cars were passing them up, "C'mon now you driving like an old feeble grandma. Yolanda, could you please speed up?" "Damn girl, I'm getting there as fast as possible", replied Yolanda. Denise apologized for snapping at her big sister, "Yo, I'm sorry. I just wanna get to the hospital so bad." The two finally arrived at the visitor's parking lot when Yolanda's cell began ringing. When she saw it was Kareem calling her back, she got a little excited as she answers, "Hey you." Kareem then asked if Denise was with her and before Yolanda could answer him. He began telling her about the news that his sister gave him about Cedric. "So they're here at the hospital", asked Yolanda. Kareem replied with a yes but in a confused voice asking her, "Y'all at the hospital already?" "Yes and I really need for you to get over here if you can 'cause I need a nice face looking at me. Your sisters and I haven't been the best of associates. Plus I have a lot to explain to you", responds Yolanda. The two hang up their phones but not before Kareem lets Yolanda know that he's in route to the hospital and they can finish talking then. She then turns to her little sister and lets her know about how the Daniels family is all here and that they are waiting on her to show up. Denise was somewhat livid because she felt that she should be the first to talk to Dr. Johnston about her husband and immediately began to blame Yolanda, "If you would have drove like you really had somewhere to be I wouldn't have to deal with them right now! You know I got a lot on my plate right now and I figured you would be a little more considerate!" Yolanda responded with strong convictions, "Hold up, hold up one second. I've been here with you since one o'clock in the morning, backing you up at all cost, and because your husband's family got to the hospital before you. You're mad at me? They've been trying to get in touch with your ass for the longest so you could meet up with them so all of you could be here. Unlike you they look at you as family and family suppose to stick together no matter what. Now I'm going look for Alonna and Shalay. You can stand your ass there looking stupid or come with me and find your husband's family." As Yolanda walked off looking for the twins she turns and almost walked directly into Shalay, who heard the whole conversation, "Oh girl, I'm sorry. I didn't see you standing there", said Yolanda. Shalay simply

82

opened her arms to Yolanda, not saying a word, and embraced her as if she was her sister, whispering in her ear, "I know we never really seen eye to eye but thank you for being here. We're gonna act like none of this happened and walk in there as a family. You don't say anything and I won't either." "I'm so sorry for the way I've been acting towards you and your family", responded Yolanda. Shalay just looked at her, smiled, and held her by the hand, "C'mon everybody's down the hall."

Sherell and Lamaj waited patiently with the Daniels family in the lobby, when Kevin and Dr. Johnston came off the elevator. "There goes my second family", stated Kevin with the biggest 'Kool-Aid smile'. Delores walked up to Kevin, held him by the face with two aged hard working hands, kissed him square on the lips and stated, "Thank God for blessing us with an angel like you." Before Kevin could introduce Dr. Johnston to the family Shalay, Yolanda, and Denise arrived just in time. "I found her", announced Shalay. As Kevin began introducing the family to Dr. Johnston, Denise couldn't take her eyes off of Sherell. "Ok, I understand that I was wrong for trying to do this without his family but why in the hell is she here", asked Denise as she whispered in Yolanda's ear. Yolanda with the most suspicious look on her face answered, "I really don't know but we're not gonna think negative at all. Didn't you say that

they been working and knowing one another for like 10 years?" Denise responded, "Actually 13 years but who's counting…" Sherell then felt it was her place to formally introduce herself to Yolanda, being that she's only heard horror stories from the twins, Kareem, and Cedric. She politely walked over with an extended hand of friendship, "Hi, I'm Sherell White, and you must be Yolanda. Kevin and I work with Cedric and he's told me a lot about you. Sorry we had to meet like this though." Yolanda just nodded in agreement, "Yes, I wish it hadn't come to this for us to meet." Sherell then turned to Denise, "Hey girl, how are you holding up?" "I'm fine. Just a little tired but I'm good", responded Denise. "Well, now that we've been all properly introduced. Shall we head to the conference room, and then we all can go up and see Mr. Daniels", stated Dr. Johnston.

Kareem was going over the floor plans for his new barber shop with the contractors when he received a phone call. He then politely excused himself noticing that it was Yolanda calling him, "Pardon me for one minute, I have to take this call." "Hey, y'all got there ok?" asked Kareem as he answered the phone. Yolanda just let out a sigh of relief as she replied, "I just needed to hear someone's voice who actually liked me and not acting like they do. You do like me as a person this time since we had our essential talk and cleared up a lot of questions about one another?" Kareem let out a loud laugh and responded, "Now that we're being honest and up front with each other. I always liked you 'cause you stood strong for what you believed in but you were; excuse my French, a little bitchy, but since we had, as you called it, our essential talk I kind of like you a little more than usual. Now does that answer your question or do I have to come

85

over there and hold your hand so you can be comfortable?" Just listening to his voice made her feel so much better but him acknowledging that he really likes her as a person and he's not doing it just to be a cordial individual felt even much better than the phone call itself. "Ok, you made your point.

Well, when will you be able to get to the hospital 'cause your family is really looking for you to be here?" asked, a now smiling, Yolanda. Kareem then told her that he's finishing up with some simple paperwork and he would be there shortly. She then told him to be careful and waited like a teenager with her first boyfriend to hang-up the phone. "Ok then, I will" answered back Kareem. After getting off the phone with Yolanda, Kareem began rushing his contractor to wrap up with the new proposals that he came up with. "Dude, I really don't care what u do. As long as it looks good, is durable, and is the same price you told me in the beginning. I gotta get to my family at the hospital" stated Kareem as he walked the gentleman to the exit door.

The Daniels family sat at a hazel colored extremely long solid wooden table, in this large conference room. Across from them were four smiling doctors including Dr. Johnston ready for the task in front of them. Dr. Johnston started introducing them one at a time, "I'd like for you to meet our cardiologist Dr. Solomon, our neurologist Dr. Nguyen and rehabilitation specialist Dr. Wilson. Right now we're here to answer any questions you may have and also assure you that we're going to do everything possible to return Cedric back to his loving family." Dr. Johnston went on in telling the Daniels' family of new scientific procedures and experimental ones with their permission that he feels will work in bringing Cedric out of his comatose state. To the family everything sounded wonderful but all Delores was concerned about at the present time was seeing her son, "I really appreciate everything all of you are doing for my son. But can I please see him now?" Delores raised herself up, put her purse on her shoulder, grabbed hold of Denise's hand and on her way out the door grabbed hold of Sherell's hand. Dr. Johnston immediately rushed in front the three ladies as their personal escort as everyone else just followed suit. As they walked down the hall Dr. Johnston informed them that Cedric's room is next. Sherell could feel Delores' grasp get tighter, knowing that the elderly mother is probably nervous and scared of what she's about to she, offered some encouraging words, "He's gonna make it out of this just fine Mama Dee." Denise then came right behind that statement, "He will mama, just you watch. We have the best doctors on the job." Sherell and Denise just looked at one another and smiled, scared and nervous themselves. Delores in turn replied, "I know he will...he has his daddy's heart." Sherell finished, "And his mama's strength. " Delores just smiled but the smile quickly went away as she entered Cedric's room. The sound of a heart monitor beeping ever so slowly, the smell of iodine and disinfectant, and the bone chilling cold in the air. The whole atmosphere felt uneasy and unwanted. Shalay opened the curtains to let in some sunshine.

Delores looked for a chair so that she can sit next to the bed holding her son. Lemaj quickly grabbed the big green cushioned chair and placed it securely behind Delores' legs. She sat down and just began talking to Cedric as if they were sitting in her living room, "Now boy what I tell you about all that reckless driving? Now look at ya...all beat up and what not. What you need to do is get up out this bed and go make me a grandchild." "I told him that last night mama", stated an out of breath Kareem, who just finished running down the hall trying to be with his family, "I'm sorry I got caught up in traffic." Delores just smiled at her baby boy,"It's ok, you're here safe now. You see your brother done got himself a fancy room? Kevin is actually worth something, besides eating up all my cooking." Everybody started laughing and Delores did her job for the day, in easing everyone's mind heavy with grief and despair. She then went on, "I know everyone has a life and responsibilities but can you please take time to at least come visit him. Talk to him, hold his hand, if it's nothing but reading a book or magazine to him, 'cause I know he can hear us. I don't want my baby in here alone." The group

agreed and the mission began.

CHAPTER 4

It's been seven and a half months since Cedric's accident,

The Daniels family, along with Sherell and Kevin, stayed focus on

their quest. Six months earlier it gained more purpose when

everyone received the news that Denise was pregnant with their

first child. Denise was spoiled by everyone, waited on hand and

foot even by Shalay and Yolanda at the same time. Yolanda's

presence became more frequent as her and Kareem's friendship

grew closer. The two spending afternoons together during the

weekend, at the hospital visiting with Cedric and even visits to

Delores' home for Sunday dinner with the rest of the family.

Sherell and Lamaj stayed a strong factor in the family, offering

their help wherever needed. Denise still had her suspicions about

Sherell but put them to the 'back burner' for the greater good of

the matter at hand for her, her husband and unborn baby's well-

being. Kevin stayed stern with Dr. Johnston and his staff, making

sure they were truly taking care of Cedric and his family's needs.

All his actions paid off when he received a call from a very excited and crying Shalay three weeks later. "He's awake! Kevin, he's awake", cried out Shalay. Kevin was at work in his office and dropped to his knees, "Thank You Jesus. Thank You. I'll be there as soon as I get off work." Before getting off the phone, Shalay made him laugh, "You will never guess how he woke up though. I was sitting in the corner and I guess I fell asleep. This boy all of a sudden starts talking and said, 'Why am I in this bed and why you look like that?' I asked him how do I look and he said 'Tore up from the floor up'" Kevin tried not to laugh but did anyway, "No he didn't" "He lucky he in the hospital", replied Shalay. Shalay then let Kevin know the rest of the family should be there shortly and they will be waiting on him. As Kevin was hanging up the phone, Sherell rushed into his office, "Did you get the news? He's awake! Alonna just called me. She's going pick up Denise and they're heading to the hospital." Kevin smiled and responded, "And so are we as soon as I put this stuff up. My dude is back!"

Alonna couldn't believe it, her brother was out of his coma and talking. She thrilled beyond imagination, her heart heavy with joy as she drove down the street to her brother's house to pick up Denise. No one really lets Denise drive anymore because first she was on bed rest, second because she was nine months pregnant and lastly her belly couldn't fit behind the wheel. As Alonna pulled up to the driveway she could see Denise and a gentleman walking out of the front door talking. The guy smiled and waved at Alonna as she did the same, then jumped into a dark green sports car. The car drove off and Denise got in the car with Alonna. Being curious Alonna couldn't help to ask, "Girl who was that cutie?" Denise laughed and replied, "Girl that was one of my co-workers passing by to check on me. He said he hadn't heard from me in a while so he passed by." Alonna thought that was sweet of him and continued heading towards the hospital to see Cedric.

Cedric was anxious to see his family but hunger was taking over his awakening body, "Nurse. Nurse, can I please get something to eat. I'm starving here." A bubbly Nursing Assistant walked into his room, "Now Mr. Daniels, I know you're feeling a little hungry but the doctors said you'll be on a strict diet for a few days." Cedric was definitely not in the mood for the liquid diet of chicken broth his doctors had in mind for him. So he just told the young lady ok and reach for the phone close to his bed. He had one person in mind that he just knew would break the rules for him and sneak in some "real" food. As the phone rang he mumbled to himself, "Reem pick up." When the phone was answered Cedric heard a female's voice. Thinking he made a mistake dialing responded, "My bad, wrong number" The woman on the other end replied, "Hey Ced, you want Reem?" Trying to catch the voice ,Cedric just told her yes and Reem immediately got on the phone, "Big Dawg! We on our way. Slow polk here took forever to get dressed." Cedric couldn't help but to ask, "You have an assistant now dude?" Kareem laughed and told him that the woman who answered the phone was Yolanda. Cedric was stunned to hear Yolanda and his little brother were friends now, let along hanging together, "If I knew this would happen I would have ended up in the hospital sooner." He could hear Yolanda in the background laughing stating, "It's not like we seeing each other Ced, geez." Kareem let Cedric know that they were just parking in the garage as he called. That's when Cedric remembered why he had called, "Damn I wanted you to stop and grab me something to eat. This soup they giving me is horrible." "I know bro but we all were given specific orders not to bring you any outside food", replied Kareem. Cedric was disappointed but understood where his little brother was coming from. When he first awakened from his seven month long slumber, besides talking to his sister. He had a real long talk with the rehabilitation specialist Dr. Wilson, who let him know that, "Just because your brain is awake and functioning properly doesn't mean your other internal organs are on the same page. You must give them a few days to catch up."

Alonna and Denise were just turning the corner in the garage when they seen Kareem and Yolanda waiting on the elevator. Alonna hurried up and parked, so they could catch the elevator together. When Yolanda seen Denise get out of the car, "Girl! You look like you bout to bust!" Denise just laughed and continued her "wobble walk" with one hand clutching her purse strap while the other rested on her hip. The four met in the elevator and headed to see Cedric. Yolanda asked if Shalay was already upstairs and Alonna informed her that she's going pick up their mother. The four headed up with nothing but joy and aspiration in their heart. As the elevator doors slowly opened, Alonna could hear her mother's voice, "They here already." She rushed down the hallway, passing smiling nurses and doctors engulfed into their art of medicines. As Alonna entered Cedric's room, her eyes fell upon her brother sitting up in his bed, one hand resting on his lap with an "IV" taped to his arm and the other hand immersed into their mother's loving hands. Cedric looked up away from his mother, "Is that my big sister Lonna? You better get over here." Alonna ran to her brother and hugged him so tight, "Girl you gone break the bones that didn't get fractured." "Oh I'm sorry", replied Alonna. Cedric just smiled and kissed her on the cheek. As he looked over his sister's shoulder he could see his happily crying wife but the impregnated image took him by surprise. Tears began filling up in the corners of his eyes as Denise walked closer and closer. Without a single word exchanged, Cedric softly embraced his wife, passionately kissed her on the lips and whispered in her ear, "Baby I'm so sorry for all of this. I should have been there for you." Denise just held onto her husband wishing to never let go of the good feeling she was having. Kareem and Yolanda made their way into the room, Kareem just stood next to his mother smiling at the beautiful site of his brother being back with them. While Yolanda sat back and enjoyed the "Kodak moment" of true family love.

The family all sat and talked to Cedric for hours. He had

a lot to catch up on, he's been asleep for months. But to him as he

hears of all the stories, it feels like he's been away for years. He

learned that both of his oldest nephews, Devin and Khori,

graduated from high school and are getting ready to attend the

University of Houston at the beginning of the school year. Cedric

also found out his youngest niece Lenelle was in the same hospital

with him for a time, after she fell off the slide at school and broke

her arm. All the cell phone photos of how the children of his

family has grown was so overwhelming and brought to reality

that his unborn child will soon be part of those photos. Cedric

looked at Denise with tears in his eyes and she couldn't help but to

ask, "Baby are you okay? Do you need me to call the nurse?" He

just smiled with, "No baby, I'm just fine. Just happy you all are

here." Then everyone in the room could hear the voice of a very

happy man, "Ya got that right. We all here now." Kevin and

Sherell stood at the door, both with delight covering their faces, seeing their co-worker and friend awake. Kevin made his way to Delores and kissed her hands, "Hello beautiful."

Kevin and Kareem just sat next to Delores in amazement at the fact that Cedric was wide awake, talking and alert to everything around him. Denise sat right at Cedric's bedside just memorizing every inch of his face. "Baby what's wrong?", asked Cedric as he leaned in to kiss her. Denise replied, "Nothing at all baby, I just miss those brown eyes and that smile. I haven't seen them in over seven months." "So do you know if we're having a boy or girl?", asked Cedric, "But it really doesn't matter as long as the baby is perfectly healthy, ten fingers and ten toes", he continued as he laid his hand on Denise's "half a beach ball" shaped pregnant belly. Before she could get out one word Dr. Wilson walked in the room, "Ok family, I hate to do it but I'm a need everybody to leave for the day because I got some work for my buddy here." Covering Cedric with an onslaught of hugs and kisses, the Daniels family and friends group exited the private room as therapist and trainers entered the room. As Denise was walking out of the room she turned and said, "How does Ashley Ja'Net Daniels sound?" "Beautiful, just like her mother", replied Cedric. His heart full of joy, Cedric was ready for anything the therapist had in store for him. His goal now was getting to his wife and soon to be here newborn baby girl.

Kareem and Yolanda were heading to her house when he received a phone call from his mother, "So son, when were you gonna tell me that you and Yolanda was a pair? I haven't seen you with none of those twerkers in like six months now. Not like I'm complaining cause Yolanda is an upgrade from your recents." Kareem burst out in a loud embarrassing laugh, "Mama! You on speaker, Yolanda is in the car with me, stop it!" Delores' innocent response, "You know better than put me on speaker, at least she knows I'm not talking bad about her, bye baby." Yolanda just blushed and put her head down laughing, "That lady is a mess but I'm glad she's in such a better mood and state of mind." Kareem parked in Yolanda's driveway, "I don't know what to do with her sometimes." Yolanda replied, "Leave her alone, she's having fun. But seriously I grilled some rib-eyes last night and you never came over to get your plate." Kareem looked at her with a strong poker-face, "Girl stop playing you know I don't turn down food. You didn't tell me to come over." The two walked in Yolanda's home jokingly bickering and still laughing at Delores' phone call. With laughter still in her voice, "Why would she think we sneaking around like we kids?" Kareem walked up to Yolanda, put his hands on her hips, pulled her close to him and now eye to eye replied, "Well we should stop playing around like two little kids then." Kareem moved in slowly waiting for a response from her but Yolanda was as scared as a teen girl in a scary movie. With her heart beating out her blouse the only words that could come out was, "What are we doing?" Kareem smiled and pressed his lips against hers and you could feel a unified exhale of ecstasy between the two.

The two simply melted into one another as Kareem's hands rolled up Yolanda's back and she held on to his firm chest. The kissing went from sweet to passionate and the two went from good friends to lovers with such a simple but ambitious gesture. Yolanda pulled his shirt over his head revealing Kareem's masculine chest and defined stomach muscles that ended in a V-shaped muscular pattern that disappeared at the top of his jeans. She paused at his belt buckle because Yolanda knew once she passes this point there's no turning back but Kareem could feel her nervousness and asked, "You ok? We can stop if you want to." Yolanda looked in his eyes, released the clamp that was holding her thick long curly hair up and began unbuttoning her blouse that exposed two of the most luscious caramel cream colored Double D's Kareem has ever laid his eyes on. She could see the marvel in his face as her blouse drops to the floor, with a sarcastic smile, "You ok? We can stop if you want to." Kareem unhooked her bra that unveiled two medium sized chocolate Hershey kisses shaped areolas which demanded him to suck on them. While the pleasure was intense for Yolanda, she tried to hold back the gasp she accidentally let out after reaching down into Kareem's jeans and coming across what she could only imagine was a hard small baby's leg. As she pulled it out, "Nope, that's not a baby leg", she whispered to herself. Kareem picked her up, holding onto Yolanda's soft ass, with her legs wrapped around him as he walked to her room and burying his face into her sweet smelling neck. Kareem whispered in her ear, "I know you taste just as good as you smell" as he laid her gently on her king sized bed and slowly eased off the rest of her clothes. Kareem stood there in awe as he enjoyed the image of this honey glazed Goddess he's about to enjoy and he did just that as the first bit of business was to see if she really taste as good as she smells. Kareem kissed his way between Yolanda's thick thighs and the two emerged into a ceremony of licks, kisses, thrust and grinding of impassioned euphoria.

Alonna and Denise were driving thru Denise and Cedric's neighborhood heading to their house when Shalay called to tell Alonna about Delores'phone call to her about Kareem and Yolanda. Alonna just started laughing, "That lady there is something else. She needs to leave that boy alone." Denise was just sitting in the car texting not really paying attention to the conversation as Alonna pulled into the driveway, "What mama do now? Y`all know she stuck in her ways." Alonna repeated what Shalay had told her, "Girl she thinks Kareem and your sister hooking up." "They just friends, besides Yolanda too 'bougie' for Kareem", replied Denise as she began to get out of the car. Alonna got off the phone with her sister and started to help Denise get inside safely, "You want me to help you with dinner or something Dee?" Denise just sat on the sofa and kicked her shoes off, "Nah girl, I'm good, you did enough. Go home and relax, cause that's what I'm about to do. I'm a get something to eat later.""Relax, with them crumb snatchers waiting on me to walk thru the door, not a chance", as Alonna was referring to her three kids at home, "Well I'm a let you get some rest" and she closed the door. Denise stayed on the sofa texting on her phone while Alonna got in her car and drove off down the street. As she heads to the traffic light she sees a familiar sight again, that dark green sports car, "Nah, that can't be the same one but it sure looks like it", she brushed it off and continued home as the sports car continued down the road.

Sherell and Lamaj made it home when Sherell received a phone call from Cedric, "Hey you, I just wanted to call you and tell you how much I really appreciate everything you have done while I was down. My mother told me how you and lil man was there for her and I just wanted to say thank you so much. It really means a lot to me." Sherell just sat there with a smile on her face, "Ced it was my pleasure and besides your mother is an angel. I'm just so glad you're back with us and about to get better." Cedric laughed, "Getting better? These doctors are working me over something serious. I'm a need recovery from them." "So are you ready to be a father? Cause I'm ready to see this pretty little girl you and Denise made. I'm so happy for you two", replied Sherell. Cedric still in shock over the pregnancy, "We've tried so many times to get pregnant and right when you stop trying, boom. I just wanna get outta this hospital before she delivers. I can't be stuck in here while she's delivering our first child." Sherell assured him that everyone will chip in to help out and that his main reason is to get healthy so that he can be there for his new family. Cedric agreed cause he knew his wife needed him more than ever. The two talked a little longer catching up on everything at work and Lamaj getting ready for high school next year when Sherell asked, "Where's Denise?" "I called the house and her cell but she's not answering. I'm figuring she's sleep", replied Cedric. Cedric chuckled, "What's up with Reem and Yolanda tho? I called him when they all were on their way to me and Yolanda answered his phone like it was hers." Sherell knew them two been hanging together a lot but thought nothing of it, "Them two just been really cool since your accident. Yolanda even came over for

Sunday dinner one time after church and we had a good time." Sherell and Cedric sat on the phone talking for awhile, enjoying each others company, "Well let me go get ready for bed, I've been relaxing in this tub for the longest talking to you Ced and this water starting to wrinkle my fingers." "My bad, go shave them hairy legs too", laughed Cedric. "Could never, these legs stay on point. Bye boy", replied Sherell as she ended the call.

Sunlight was peaking between the curtains in Yolanda's bedroom waking Kareem up from a peacefully sound sleep. He glanced over to a beautiful sight of Yolanda laying there like a glamour model as the light kissed her flawless honey amber toned skin and he thought to himself, "I could really get use to this shit here. Dammit this girl is so fine." With one finger he slid her hair back away from her face and kissed her lips, "Good morning Miss Patton, you want some breakfast?" Yolanda awakened with a smile on her face as she heard that deep baritone voice stroked her ear drum, "You just gonna kiss this 'morning breath' and not give me a chance to clean up. I don't know if you know how to cook yet, I don't do fast food breakfast." "Girl you are doubting my skills? I'm a super master chef, watch me work", replied Kareem as he continued, "Besides you lucky I kissed your lips under your nose and not the ones under your belly button." Yolanda shivered thinking about the phenomenal chain of events that took place last night that brought them to this present moment. Kareem got out of bed, slipped on his jeans and pulled his dreads into one tight group. As he was walking out of the bedroom Yolanda just sat up in the bed looking at him, "Lawd, I could really get use to this, goodness he is so fine", was the first thought that ran thru her head. Kareem made himself comfortable in the kitchen cause his mother taught him at an early age how to cook, "You really know your way around a kitchen, I see", acknowledged Yolanda as she walked in covered in a short silk kimono. "I told you I'm a pro in the kitchen", replied Kareem as he sliced up some oranges and watching his pancakes cook in the skillet. Yolanda was enjoying this moment but she had concerns as to where it's going, "I don't want to spoil any of this cause I'm loving every bit of it but what are we doing, where do we go from here cause I definitely can't just go back to being buddy buddy after last night. Now don't get me wrong I'm not trying to get you to commit into a relationship or anything, I just don't wanna be your jump off." Kareem put his finger over her lips, "Shhhhh, eat your pancakes and bacon. Do you like cream and sugar in your coffee or would you rather some orange juice?" Yolanda slightly smiled and reached for the orange juice. She's use to having control and dominating any situation but being controlled in a sense and letting the dominating be done to her was a bit intriguing, something she didn't realize she would like. The couple sat at the table, enjoyed breakfast and good conversation in the early morning hours.

    Cedric woke up to his nurse checking his vitals, "I'm all good nurse lady", she laughed and walked out the room. Cedric hadn't talk to his wife all night and he needed to hear her voice, "She gone wake up and talk to me", as he dialed her number.

Denise answered the phone out of breath, "Hello handsome, you up early. I'm sorry I missed your calls last night, after I got home, I fell right to sleep. Your daughter is draining me." Cedric couldn't do anything but smile after hearing about his child being so active already. He guaranteed Denise that he will be out of the hospital before she delivers and be there for her more than ever, "Baby get yourself healthy and strong, me and Ashley have our whole lives to be with you", replied Denise. The two talked about what they wanted to do after the baby arrives, Denise told him how Kareem and the twins have already painted the baby's room and decorated, she told him how Yolanda has been buying clothes every week bringing them over and how anxious his mother has been to see her new grandchild. Denise then asked him one question no one has asked since the accident, "Baby do you remember anything about the accident?" Cedric's response baffled her but comforted her all the same, "Baby to be honest it was kinda weird cause I remember a big black truck and then I was hanging upside down in water. My dad, my uncle David and my

110

grandpa pulled me out of the water and they brought me to my grandma that just held on to me. She kept repeating 'Here they come baby. Here they come' and after that everything is really fuzzy. Now I know all the people that I just mentioned is dead and have been for some time now so I know they weren't there at the accident but that's who I remember being there." "Baby they say everyone has Guardian Angels, it looks like you have four of them. But from what the police report and the doctors say what happened, you are pretty close to the events that took place. I'm blown away that you can remember all that after all that has happened", replied Denise. "Well baby Dr. Johnston just walked in the room with a smile on her face, she probably got a bunch of crazy exercises for me to do again, pray for me cause I think she trying to kill me", laughed Cedric. Denise giggled, "Boy stop it, she getting you better, I'm a see you soon." The two hung up the phone and Cedric prepared himself for today's workout, "What we got today Doc?" Dr. Johnston smiled and handed him a folder with Cedric's name printed in the corner. The top papers were different exercises he had to do, the next few pages were scheduled visits to her private office and the last two pages all had printed at the top "Discharge for Cedric Daniels". With excitement in his voice, "Doc please tell me this is not a dream, I can really go home today, like really go home to my family." Dr. Johnston just nodded her head, "Yes Mr. Daniels, you have recovered with flying colors, faster than any patient I have ever encountered and I feel you are ready. Now I'm not saying jump right back into normal routine but I believe you are truly ready to go home to your family. I'll see you again in a week and after that every two weeks with me and my psychiatric staff but you have to do your exercises everyday. Deal?" Cedric couldn't believe he was being released from the hospital and didn't know who to call first but he knew he had to get home by any means. He didn't want to call Denise because he wanted to surprise her and his family, so he called the one person he knew would be ready to come get him at any moment, Kevin.

Alonna stopped by Sherell like she usually does every weekend but she seen a sight that was way too familiar and a little eerie. The same dark green sports car she seen in front of Denise and Cedric's house was parked in front of Sherell's house this time. As she got out of her car the same handsome guy she seen was walking out of Sherell's front door. Baffled at the coincidence for a second time she wondered who this stranger really is, "Well hello again sir, we know too many of the same people but we don't know each other. Hi, I'm Alonna Daniels." He smiled and shook her hand, "I know who you are, you're Denise's sister-in-law, I'm Jamal A. Green." "Yeah my sperm donor. Come inside Alonna, bye Jamal", replied Sherell. Alonna with a confused look on her face didn't really know what to do after that but headed inside as Sherell closed the door behind her. Alonna never met Lamaj's father in the thirteen years she has been knowing them and now kind of realized why, "So that was him? Don't look like you really like him much, I'm just saying." "Yeah that's his dad. Bastard comes over maybe every other month filling my son head with pipe dream promises and then I gotta repair it all when he breaks Lamaj's heart with some bullshit excuse", replied Sherell. Alonna then told her that she seen him a few days ago by Denise that's how she recognized him, "Yeah, he's one of the Lieutenant Security Guards at NASA so I guess they sent him over there, I don't know girl", replied Sherell. Sherell went on about Jamal, "Girl I was whipped behind that dude but the real him showed up when I told him I was pregnant and poof he disappears on days end. I finally got tired of the lies and excuses and made myself disappear but as you can see he found me. Big head bastard even friend requested me on social media talking about so we can keep in touch for the sake of our child." Alonna just sat back and listened knowing she has had her share of disappointments in men but found a real good one in her fiancé Steven, Deshanae's father. "Ok girl, enough about him where's my handsome lil man at?", asked Alonna. Lamaj walked up to Alonna with a bowl of cereal in his hand, kissed her on the cheek and went sat on the sofa to look at TV. Sherell was disturbed by how Jamal handles his role as a father but Lamaj has grown to accept his father's broken promises as the norm. He has grown more than she knows in that aspect. Lamaj uses his father's inconsistencies as motivation into becoming better person, son and future father, "Auntie Lonna did mama ever tell you how she came up with my name? You gotta hear it." "Girl when he came out, he looked just like his paw but I refused to name my child after him. I wanted my son to be the total opposite of his father so I spelled his name backwards. Also Jamal full name is Jamal Ashley Green, J.A.G. and Lamaj full name is Lamaj Anthony White, L.A.W. cause I want my son to be the correction of my fuck-ups", replied Sherell. Alonna and Lamaj just looked at Sherell and both fell out laughing. Alonna couldn't believe she had a complete story behind the purpose of a name all the way down to the initials, "Girl he really did a number on you. Well we gone forget all about all of this today. You ready to head out to the store?" Sherell grabbed her purse, told Lamaj she'll be back later today so they could go visit Cedric in the hospital and the two ladies got in the car and headed off.

CHAPTER 5

Kevin and Cedric were driving up his street, the closer Cedric got to his home the faster his heart raced and he hadn't been to his house in over seven months, all he wanted to do was walk thru his front door. "Dude I cant believe they released you so fast, Dee gone lose her mind when she sees you walk thru the door", expressed Kevin. Cedric couldn't believe it himself but he wasn't gonna question Dr. Johnston's decision to discharge him and he couldn't wait to see his wife's face, "Stop! I need a big favor Kev, can you turn around and go to the store for me." Kevin made a U-turn and headed to the store as asked, "What's wrong and which store?" Cedric wanted to surprise his wife with some flowers along with his arrival home. He and Kevin walked into a nearby grocery store when Kevin was telling him about his sister Shalay, "Dude I took your sister up on her offer." "Oh, you finally gonna be her next baby daddy", replied Cedric. Kevin laughed, "No fool. She wanted to have her hotel host our next

Medical Conference and I think it's gonna be a good look for the both of us." Cedric was pleased his sister was moving up in her business ventures, "That's a good look for both of you for real. Maybe you could take her out for dinner afterwards", chuckled Cedric. "Yeah the same time you and Sherell go on a date", replied Kevin. The guys both laughed at each others comment as Cedric gathered two dozen red and yellow roses. Kevin mentioned to Cedric if he knew that yellow roses mean friendship and Cedric let him know that he knew that but yellow is Denise's favorite color. The guys headed to the register when Cedric realized he didn't have his wallet and Kevin was more than happy to pay for the roses, he grabbed a bottle of wine to top it all off. They then made their way back to Cedric's house, "Kevin, this whole ordeal has opened my eyes that life truly is short and can be gone in a split second. When they say your life flash before your eyes they lied cause all I seen was a bright flash of light and boom. I heard some voices, then there was darkness and next I was waking up in a hospital like it was the next day but in actuality months had

117

went by. From now on I'm a enjoy every bit, everyday, every hour and every minute." Kevin responded, "Nah dawg, those bright lights you seen was the headlights on that Mack truck you jumped in front of and it used you as a hood ornament. I feel you on living life to the fullest dawg, I'm always looked at as the carefree rich guy who doesn't have to work, but that's because I've seen what just working and paying bills can do to a person. Now I'm not saying you gotta travel the world or go to exotic islands every other month but you do have to enjoy life and enjoy it with someone you love. Cedric, I envy you cause you have that right now homie."

As Kevin pulled up to Cedric's house he seen a dark green sports car parked in front, "Now that's a nice Hellcat right there, you know that's one of the fastest street legal cars out right now, who's ride?" Cedric never seen the car before and figured it wasn't for anyone he knew personally. The guys just got out of Kevin's car and made their way to the front door, Cedric went to his secret flower pot that hides the extra house key and Kevin

stood back admiring the sports car. Cedric slowly unlocked the

front door so to not alarm Denise with the roses clutched in his

hand and as he got close to the den he heard sounds that he's use

to hearing only during a highly sexual encounter with his wife but

he wasn't involved this time. Kevin heard the sounds also and

instantly knew something was wrong but moved to slow to stop

Cedric from making it to the den. The sounds of moans, grunts

and slurping filled the room as the roses fell to the floor and

Cedric stood in utter shock in the doorway of his den. Kevin

walked up behind him and his eyes fell upon Cedric's pregnant

wife Denise on her knees in front of a guy sitting on the sofa with

his pants at his ankles giving him some amazing oral pleasure.

Denise and the guy both had their eyes closed enjoying the

moment as the guy reached and grabbed a handful of Denise's hair

as she took more of his manhood into her mouth. Denise gagged

as she forced his member deep in her throat, stroking his shaft

with both of her hands she raised up off of him and smiled

knowing she's pleasing his every need. When she looked up she was startled to see two male figures standing in the doorway but when her eyes focused on one of the male figures she realized it was Cedric staring at her with a face of complete disgust. The guy on the sofa put his hand on the back of Denise's head and began to try and feed her his hardened organ, "Nah bitch, put this dick back in your mouth." "Yeah bitch, put his dick back in your mouth, don't stop because of us", replied Cedric as he walked into the den. The guy jumped off the sofa pulling his pants up while Denise stayed knelt down in pure distress as fear filled her body. Denise slowly raised herself to her feet as to not make any sudden moves like she was standing in the room with a ravenous tiger. Kevin stood at the doorway stuck with his eyes focused on his friend, hoping he doesn't do anything rash. As Cedric walked in he noticed the guy's face, "You're the security guard. Bitch you fucking the help?! So security guard dude, how's her skills? That shit felt good, right? Yo shit must be huge bruh cause this bitch ain't ever gag giving me head." Denise cried out, "Cedric, wait! I didn't…" Cedric stopped her, "Didn't know I was coming home right now? You fucking the security guard but you always accusing me of cheating while you're the one fucking around." Cedric turns to the guy, "Say dude, what's your name? I have no problems with you, you just doing what any single man would do, I just wanna know your name." The guy replied, "Jamal Green" Cedric laughed in Denise's face, "Wow, do you really know who this is bitch or are you just fucking retarded as fuck!"

Kevin cell started ringing, "Hello hello" It was Kareem on the other end looking for Cedric, "What's up Kev, I don't mean to bother you but have you talked to Cedric? I'm at the hospital and they just told me that he was discharged today. I tried calling Denise but nobody answering their phones" "Please get to Ced's house now. Some shit is about to fucking go down, your brother's fine but I don't know if I can hold him", answered Kevin. Kareem didn't ask not one more question and ended the call. He was with Yolanda at the hospital and let her know they need to get to

Cedric's house as fast as they can. Yolanda concerned her sister has gone into labor immediately called Denise as Kareem sped down the street. Kareem scared his brother was hurt or worse didn't know what to think. He called Shalay to let her know what's going on and told her to call Alonna also. Kareem was almost in tears, scared to see what's going on at his brother's house, "Baby what's wrong? What exactly did Kevin say?", asked Yolanda. "He just said to get to the house now and that something is about to happened", responded Kareem.

The closer they got to the house the more nervous the both of them got as Kareem made his way thru the neighborhood. Yolanda sitting up in the car ready to jump out had already taken off her seat-belt, she could see the house approaching. Kareem parked and the two got out of the car and could almost immediately hear arguing coming from the house . Yolanda ran to the front door to find it wide open and she could see Kevin standing in between Cedric and Denise. She seen her sister crying and immediately reached out to her, "What's wrong baby? What happened? You not in labor are you?" Cedric's response confused Yolanda even more, "Yeah tell your sister what's really going on, what I just walked up on. SPEAK! You don't have nothing in your mouth this time!" Kareem walked up to Kevin and asked him what happened before they got there. When Kevin started to recap what had brought them to this moment Denise blurted out, "STOP TELLING MY BUSINESS!" "Why not, you don't want your sister to know you like to have Jamal's dick in ya mouth", loudly replied Cedric. Yolanda loss for words looked at Denise with all sorts of confusion and sadness covering her face, she didn't want to believe the words coming from Cedric but the sight of the gentleman she's never seen before sitting on the sofa was an ominous clue that all of the accusations were true. Kareem and Kevin tried to calm Cedric down by pulling him in the kitchen away from the situation but Cedric forcefully held them off, "No, I need this bitch and that nigga up out my damn house before I move anywhere. Is that baby even mine bitch? Huh, ANSWER

ME!" Suddenly the group all wondered if the unborn child was actually for Cedric or was it for Jamal. The look on Denise and Jamal's faces answered everyone's assumption, at that point confusion and sadness instantly left Yolanda and she was engulfed with uncontrollable anger toward her younger sister as the sound of an open hand slap filled the room. Kareem ran over to Yolanda as she reprimanded her little sister as if she was sixteen years old, "Have you fucking lost your damn mind! You're a married woman! Let alone a black woman! We have it hard enough just trying to make it in this world with people looking at us as being beneath them and Yo ass go and do exactly what they think all of us do. You not only disrespected yourself but you disrespected everything mommy has taught us, everything we have fought to overcome. You go and dishonor your vows like some fucking tramp!" Jamal gets up from the sofa and consoles Denise as she falls to her knees crying while her sister continues to batter her with her raid of aggressive rants.

Kareem knew he had to get Yolanda out of the room before she says anymore but he was concerned for his brother also. Kareem walked up to Jamal, "Dude I think you and her need to leave, I don't know where but I know y'all need to get outta here." Jamal helped Denise to her feet as she looked her sister square in the face, "So you're gonna just take his side and not even hear me out?" "There's no explanation for what you've done Denise, none at all baby", replied Yolanda. A cloud of resentment enveloped Denise as she gathered herself, "So you finally get you some young dick and all of a sudden you a certified Daniels now? Just fuck me? Your own flesh and blood can't get any type of respect from you?", scolded Denise. Yolanda's face was defeated as she sat down and leaned back into a nearby lounge chair, "You know what, as my only sister I will give you that. I will give you the opportunity to tell me how the hell all of this took place. Please tell me Cedric was physically abusive, that he cheated on you repeatedly, that he just didn't care about your well-being. Please tell me he did at least one of those things and I can understand why you got pregnant by another man." Denise and Jamal just quietly walked out the front door, everybody was perplexed as they watched them get into Jamal's car. Cedric walked off into the kitchen, opened the cabinet, pulled out a bottle of top shelf tequila and asked, "Anybody want to join me in my homecoming slash divorce?" Yolanda stood next to him and laid her head on his shoulder, "I am so sorry this happened to you Ced, you did not deserve this.""The funny thing about it all is that she's gonna name the baby Ashley and I was gonna carry on as she's mine, not knowing a thing. Jamal's full name is Jamal Ashley Green. You wanna know why I know this? The woman that she would always accuse me of having a fling with, Sherell. Jamal is her son's father and now he's about to father a child with my wife. What's the irony of that shit?", cried Cedric. Kevin and Kareem didn't know how to handle the situation as Cedric and Yolanda just comforted each other over the actions of the one person they didn't think would ever hurt them. The two men walked outside to get some air, leaving Yolanda and Cedric inside to themselves and

Kareem had to know what exactly happened. Kevin then told him every single detail of the event and Kareem couldn't believe the words that was coming out of his mouth. "So you're telling me they didn't hear y`all walk in the house?", asked Kareem. Kevin just shook his head no and continued on with the story.

Cedric and Yolanda were sitting in the kitchen attempting to drink their sorrows away as they still couldn't believe what just happened. Yolanda kept looking at her cell phone hoping to see her little sister's number flash across her screen. "So how did you end up getting out of the hospital anyways? Who you bribe to get released?", laughed Yolanda. Cedric chuckled and told her how Dr. Johnston felt it would be better for his recovery to finish at home. "Guess I'll be bugging y'all everyday to do these exercises and therapeutic workouts", said Cedric as he showed her the medical forms the doctor gave him. "You won't be bugging us Ced", replied Yolanda. Cedric couldn't help but to ask about her and his little brother, "So is it true about you and Kareem? I'm not against it at all but I'm just wondering what brought this funny relationship on?" Yolanda began to tell him how her and Kareem started talking to one another everyday after his accident. She actually admitted how she felt about his family at first and how Kareem opened her eyes to the truth. Yolanda even apologized for her wrongful evaluations of his siblings, that she can in fact see why Sherell and Kevin embrace this family as if it were their own. She then went on to telling him about his mother's phone call and how funny it was that Delores cold see the connection before they even knew they would be an item. The two laughed but Cedric knew his siblings were a little rough around the edges to a blind eye, "Yeah those three are like an enigma, you can't quite understand them but you are drawn to them. Now that old lady is a force to be reckoned with, she loves her kids to death but she's straight old school, that tough love sort of speak. I think I'm the only normal one." Yolanda then remembered that Kareem called his sisters right before they got to the house, "I may need to leave cause Alonna and Shalay should be on their way here after Reem's phone call and I don't want them to have any animosity towards me over all this nonsense." Cedric assured her that her place is right where she's at, that she need not worry about his sisters holding any ill felt feelings for her. Yolanda smiled and poured two glasses of water, "Well let me sober you up before they get here cause I'm not gone get fussed at for having you tipsy straight out the hospital." "I don't think anybody will be concerned about me being a little inebriated after today", gestured Cedric as he took a big swallow from the glass. Kevin walked inside with Kareem following behind, "I just realized ole buddy is kinda corny. His car green and his last name Green." Cedric burst out laughing, "Dude it took you all that time to catch that, like really? You been drinking?" "Not yet but I plan on to", replied Kevin as he poured him and Kareem two short glasses of Tequila.

Alonna, Sherell and Shalay were almost at Cedric's house when Sherell's cell started buzzing, it was a text from her son,

"Mama, dad just texted me and told me I'm about to have a little sister." She texted him back, "Wow, you ok with that son?" "Of course, I'm bout to be a big brother", replied Lamaj. Sherell couldn't believe Jamal told her son that news before consulting with her first. Little did she know the news of the baby is about to shock all three of them in the car. Alonna parked her car behind Kareem's and immediately saw an unexpected image of her brothers laughing through the large living room window. "What the hell is going on?", asked Shalay. Confused herself, Alonna just replied, "I don't know but we bout to find out." As they got closer to the door, music and laughter continued to get louder, puzzling the women even more considering the phone call they received earlier. Shalay walked in first to see Kevin sitting on the floor crying laughing, "Mama Dee said you know better than to put her on speakerphone." Kareem replied, "Dawg that lady is a mess, she gave zero fucks that day but y'all should have seen the look on Yolanda's face though." Kevin kept laughing and looked up to see Shalay standing next to him, "Dang girl! You part ninja, how you gone just sneak up on a brother like that?" The ladies all were rattled at the party style appearance as they stood looking at everyone else enjoying themselves. "Kareem, you called me frantic, sounding like something was wrong with Ced and got us all scared but y'all here clowning?", asked Shalay. "My bad my bad, we were all caught up in the moment and it was my fault", replied Cedric as he began walking toward the ladies, "They all were trying to make me feel better after all the bullshit that went down earlier with your soon to be ex-sister-in-law." Cedric made his way to Sherell, staring her in her big brown eyes, "This is something I been wanting to do for the past ten years." Cedric kissed Sherell so passionate that the room went silent and it was like everyone in it disappeared except for them. "I've been having feelings for you for the longest and I refused to take advantage of you cause I cared for you so much but you understood all the same. We never crossed that line but today is a brand new day and you are the one person I want to start fresh with", acknowledged Cedric as he held Sherell close to him. "Alright now, get it Ced", publicized Yolanda. "I'm not totally against your actions but what the fuck is going on in here and Yolanda, you cool with this? The hell!", announced Alonna. The group started chuckling and laughing at the three baffled women as they tried to understand what exactly was going on. Cedric started telling them how he was released from the hospital and he wanted to surprise everyone by calling after he gets home. He told them how he wanted to surprise his wife first with some flowers and the shock he received. He then told the three women the horrendous site he walked in on with Kevin and as the words began to flow out of his mouth, everyone could hear the hurt in his voice. Kareem even tried to stop him but Cedric needed to get it all out now considering he didn't really want to talk about it anymore. The news floored the women as Cedric continued his terrible story and Sherell put everything together as she heard that Jamal was the guy that Denise was having a relationship with. "Wait one minute, that motherfucker called and told my son he's about to have a little sister. Tell me that shit ain't true Ced?", asked Sherell. Yolanda confirmed her thoughts, "Girl I'm just as confused and pissed as you are. I can't believe my sister stooped to that level. To disrespect her marriage like that, let alone herself by getting pregnant for another man and was gonna live with that lie. She literally had no remorse in her face." The group all sat in astonishment of the events wondering what's next and Cedric could see it on everyone's face, "Hey! This suppose to be a celebration of my homecoming dammit! Y'all sitting around like somebody stole ya puppy. I don't know about y'all but I wanna enjoy this day." "Enough said", replied Kevin as he turned up the radio.

Yolanda was enjoying everyone but in the back of her mind she knew she needed to talk to her sister and clear the air. She stepped away from the group and went in the backyard to call Denise. The phone was ringing and Yolanda was trying to get her words together but there was no answer as the answer service came on. She just left a message hoping her little sister would listen and call her back, "Dee I know you're upset and probably don't wanna hear my voice but I want you to know I love you regardless. You will always be my little sister and I will always be there for you, no matter what." Yolanda sat down and began to quietly cry to herself as everything began to hit her at once. She started to realize the family she has grew to love and cherish just got flipped upside down and she was stuck right in the middle of it this time. She's usually the one that stands off and only concerns herself with Denise's well-being but now she's invested in the family, not just because of Kareem but because she has grown to love and respect the twins also along with Delores. "I can't believe this shit is happening right now", whispered Yolanda. The thought of losing her sister scared her because they were so close and Yolanda just wanted to hear her little sister's voice to make sure she was alright. She continued to call Denise's number only to get an answering service but then received a text message that read, "Please stop calling me. You made your decision and I have made mine, we have nothing to talk about. My only concern is me and my child." Yolanda dropped her phone in tears, she couldn't believe the words she just read and she knew how stubborn her sister is so she didn't try to text her back knowing her message would fall on deaf ears. Kareem seen Yolanda sitting outside and knew something had to be wrong but didn't know how to approach the situation, should he let her be or should he engage. Cedric walked up behind him, "Boy if you don't go out there and talk to her. I really think she needs you right now, go 'head."

Cedric watched as Kareem stepped out on the backyard deck and Yolanda grasped onto him crying on his chest. He couldn't hear what was being said but he knew his brother was a much needed shoulder for Yolanda to lean on at the time. Cedric left them to their conversation as he walked off to talk to Sherell alone, "Hey you." Sherell smiled but kept her distance. She explained that she doesn't want Cedric to just jump in on trying to be with her in a relationship, that she wants him to heal from the hurt first, get himself together and then they can talk about maybe working on something special. As hard as it was for Sherell to step back from what she truly wants, she knew it was for the better for Cedric. Cedric knew she meant well and understood he needs to get a lot of affairs in order before he even tries to start a new relationship. The two stood in the living room as Cedric looked over everything in the room, "I know one thing I'm definitely doing is getting rid of this sofa set. Dude naked ass and balls were all on my damn sofa." Sherell tried not to laugh at Cedric's joke but couldn't help herself as she put her head on his shoulder, "You stupid for real. That's the first thing you think of?" The two friends laughed as Cedric explained how he wants to just start all over and forget today. He admitted that he feels bad for Yolanda because her and Kareem may grow apart from one another behind he and Denise's sudden split. "If it's meant to be trust me nothing will come between them. Besides they're cute together, I'm happy for Reem", responded Sherell as she pointed toward Kevin and Shalay, "But what are we gonna do with them two? They been flirting for years and I don't think Kev realize that

Shalay is serious as hell. She gone put it on him." Cedric laughed, "Kev, you not trying to become my brother-in-law over there are you?" Shalay giggled, "He ain't ready bro, he ain't ready." Cedric sat back and just admired everyone that was there for him and realized through all of the excitement and commotion, he hadn't talk to his mother since he been home. When he called her Delores was ecstatic that her oldest son was finally home but she knows her child and asked the one question all parents ask, "You don't sound like you, what's wrong?" Cedric just smiled as he heard his mother ask but gave her the watered down version that he was just tired from all the excitement of finally being home and he promised her he will be by first thing in the morning.

CHAPTER 6

It's been a week since Cedric been home and he was getting himself back on track. An early morning two mile walk through the neighborhood felt good as he focused on how he's ready to get his life back together. Yolanda still hadn't heard from her little sister and every call or text she sent were simply ignored with no response or reply. Kareem was days away from his Grand Opening of his new shop and was ready to get started on his new adventure. Shalay and Kevin were finalizing their convention program as Alonna was helping Delores redecorate her garden as she always does every Spring. Sherell was sitting at her desk when she received a call from Cedric, "Hey girlie, what you doing? I was wondering if you wanted to go to lunch today cause I have a doctor's appointment out by you." Sherell happily agreed to the meeting, "That sounds like a winner but the question is are you paying homie?" Cedric laughed, "Girl as handsome as I am, you should be paying to be seen with me." The two laughed as

Cedric started to get himself back to his house but he seen a discouraging image parked in front of his home, "Hey Rell, let me call you back right quick." Jamal was knocking on his front door as Cedric was walking up, "Say man, what you want? She ain't here." Jamal turned around chuckling, "Nigga I know that, she sent me over here to get some of her stuff." Cedric was full of instant rage as he focused on the villainous smile Jamal carried the closer he got, "Nigga you gone have to come back later today cause I got shit I gotta do and yo ass ain't walking thru my damn house." Jamal then let Cedric know he knew where everything is that he needs to get as if he knew the house like he knew the back of his hand. Cedric still was adamant that Jamal was not stepping in his home as Jamal's last statement was like a knife in his stomach. Jamal backed down and let Cedric know he'll be back later that afternoon to pick up Denise's items and not to forget her shoe collection or makeup bags in the walk-in closet on the vanity. "Nigga , you need to get the fuck off my property right now", replied Cedric. Jamal smiled and drove off as Cedric went inside enraged that Denise had another man in his house as if it was his own. He thought to himself, "How could she fix her mouth to accuse me of having an affair but she's literally dating another guy while she's married to me", as he gathered Denise's clothes out of the closet and stuffed them in large black garbage bags.

Time got away from Cedric as he attempted to clear away anything that reminded him of Denise. He cleared out the closets, dresser drawers, cabinets and even pictures off the walls of Denise as he carried it all one large bag at a time to the front lawn. Cedric just happened to look at his cell to see what time it was when he noticed that he missed a call from Sherell, "Damn, it's too late for lunch now." He called her back to apologize for standing her up and let her know what he was dealing with at the time. Sherell was shocked that Jamal actually showed up to Cedric's house but was more concerned about how her friend was handling the situation, "You good? I'm about to get off in a bit and I can pass over." Cedric declined the visit but told her he'll call her later today when he think she's home. Cedric ended the call and finished grabbing the last of the bags to bring outside. He sat on his porch waiting for Jamal to come back watching people go about their lives not knowing the ordeal he's going through inside. Cedric knew it was a matter of time before he would need to get a lawyer to legally conclude this already terminated relationship of a marriage. He called his friend Kevin for any suggestions of a good lawyer and Kevin let him know he's going to get right on the task for him. Kevin tried to uplift his friend's spirit by giving Shalay a lot of praise on how she handled the missions he had for her with the upcoming convention and how she managed to take care of it all, "That girl plays around when we chilling but when it's time to take care of business she don't play at all, I see why she's the GM of that hotel." Cedric sat there proud as he heard of his sister's accomplishments at work, "Yeah she's good at what she does. I'm glad y'all hooked up on the project."

Yolanda was on her way to Kareem's shop when she got a call from an unknown number and thinking it was one of her teachers from the school, "Yes, Principal Patton." It was Jamal on the other end, he apologized for calling her and told her some news she's been waiting for awhile. He explained that Denise was still pretty upset over their falling out but he also felt that she should know that her little sister gave birth to her daughter two days ago. Yolanda was so excited but sadden all the same because her own sister didn't call her with this lovely news. Jamal told her what hospital Denise was in and that he think it's a good idea that she goes to visit her. Yolanda was eager to go see her sister that she almost forgot that she was suppose to meet Kareem. She called him to give him the news of the birth and that she won't be able to see him until later. Kareem totally understood, "No problem baby, tell her I said congratulations. I'll see you when you get home." Yolanda headed to the hospital joyous but scared because she didn't know how Denise would handle seeing her since their last interaction together. She walked up to the nurse's station, asked for Denise Daniels' room and the nurse pointed her in the right direction. Yolanda slowly walked to the room and as she seen her little sister sitting up on her bed with her newborn safely cradled in her arms, the tears began to flow. Denise seen her sister standing at the door and didn't say one word, her eyes alone said come in and sit down. The two sat there silent for a minute as Yolanda just gazed at the beauty of her niece. Denise then made an ultimate gesture with her two day old daughter and placed her in her sister's arms, "Ashley, say hello to Auntie Landa." Yolanda knew right at that point everything was right with her and her sister and that she would do anything for this little girl in her arms.

Cedric almost gave up on waiting on Jamal to arrive when he seen a bright green pick-up pull up to his house. Jamal got out and looked at all the black trash bags, "Nigga you couldn't put the stuff in boxes, damn." "You lucky I didn't just throw the shit on the ground. What you need to be concerned with is grabbing yo bitch shit and getting the fuck from in front my house", replied Cedric as he stood boiling with intense animosity watching Jamal's every move. As Jamal placed the last bag in the back of the truck he turned to Cedric, "Nigga you standing there looking butt hurt for real. You must have really thought she was yours and only yours. That pussy been mine, I was just letting you borrow it." Cedric stepped off his porch, "Dude yo best out is to get the fuck from in front my face before we really have problems." Jamal laughed out loud, "I don't want no smoke" , but as he turned, "Bitch ass nigga ain't gone do shit." Cedric heard the comment and instantly struck Jamal in the side of his head and then kicked him in his lower back. When Jamal fell to the ground stunned, Cedric's attacks continued with a barrage of heavy rights and stinging lefts. Jamal managed to get Cedric off of him with a timely landing right between the blitz of punches he was receiving. The two men rose to their feet and engaged into a systematic downpour of punches, elbows and jabs. In the midst of being knocked to the ground for a second time, Jamal remembered he had a board in the back of the truck. He got up to

retrieve the board and made a beeline toward Cedric with all

intent to inflict as much pain as he could. Swinging as if he was a

pro baseball player, Jamal struck Cedric twice on the arm. But his

third swing was caught by Cedric and countered with a

thunderous right cross to the left side of his face. Jamal's body

then went limp to the ground for the third and final time as Cedric

stood firm over him, "Get yo bitch ass up and get the fuck!" Jamal

slowly stood to his feet, managed to get in his truck as he assessed

his swelling jawline, started the engine and drove off. Cedric

walked inside as his neighbors tried to understand what just took

place. He got a wet cold towel and wiped the blood from his

knuckles when the doorbell rung. Cedric believing it was Jamal

back for round two grabbed a bat resting in the corner and headed

to the door with anger filling his eyes. He swung the front door

open to find Sherell standing there in some tight white cotton

yoga shorts and a wife-beater. The image of Cedric standing in

front of her bloody nose, cut lip, swollen eye and blood stained

145

shirt was not what she was expecting, "Ced, what the hell happened?" Cedric explained to her what took place a few minutes before she arrived and that he just wants to be alone right now. Sherell refused to leave her friend and stayed to help mend his wounds as she grabbed the ice tray out of the freezer. She made an ice pack, placed it on Cedric's eye and then tended to his cut lip by softly wiping the blood from it. Sherell could see he was still emotionally agitated so she suggested that Cedric go upstairs to take a shower, he complied and did just that.

While Cedric was upstairs showering, Sherell began cleaning up the blood stained towels, putting them in the linen closet, putting things back in their place and then she started pouring them both a glass of ice tea from the fridge. She headed upstairs figuring Cedric was finished showering and walked toward his room. As she walked in, Cedric was walking out of his bathroom still dripping wet with a large white towel wrapped around his waist and neither looked away from one another.

Sherell stated she was bringing him something to drink so he could take an aspirin for pain. Cedric looked at Sherell standing in his bedroom with her thick smooth thighs exiting from her white shorts, delectable plump cleavage pushing its way up out from her shirt and luscious lips slightly glistening in the light. He couldn't deny himself anymore and as he walked toward her his towel fell to the floor. He pressed his naked body against her as he pressed his lips to hers and they both secured themselves into a passionate kiss. Sherell knew she couldn't resist it again like before as Cedric's hands moved down to the small of her back. She seemed to melt when he kissed her again but this time Cedric picked her up and her legs instantly wrapped around him. He walked to the bed, slowly laid Sherell down and he started to ease her shorts off of her as she began to pull her top over her head. "What are we doing?", was the only words she could get out as he kissed her behind her ear, then her collarbone, then made his way to her erect nipples a top her grand double deez and they demanded he suck them. Sherell enjoyed the pleasure of his warm mouth on her breast but she could feel his strong hands slide between her thighs and begin to massage her moistened clit. Chills went thru her as he moved from her breast, to her navel, then his tongue slid across her hips as he made himself comfortable between her thick soft thighs. It felt as if his tongue grew twice its size as it parted her smooth waxed lips and rested flat against her jumping clitoris. Long strokes of his tongue on her clit became shorter and shorter until his tongue was a whirlwind of vibrating twirls and flicks. Sherell's body electrified into an orgasmic spasm while Cedric's tongue filled her up. After indulging himself in his juicy appetizer, he climbed deep between Sherell's captivating thighs and pressed his engorged member deep inside her. A gasp and then an array of goosebumps crawled up her back as she could feel an endless amount of harden muscle simply submerged itself between her moist soften pussy lips. A sexual energy cord was made and the bond was immensely strong between them.

Yolanda left the hospital after visiting with her sister and a joy surrounded her as she got into her car. Her and Denise resolved their misunderstanding as Denise explained how the affair all started. She told her she knew it was wrong but she fell for Jamal over time as the affection got stronger everyday. Denise told her how Jamal would make her feel good with simple "Good morning beautiful" or "Thinking about you" text. Things that seem to fall at the wayside when it involved Cedric. She even mentioned that she started to become more distant with Cedric the closer her and Jamal got and that the relationship never started off sexual. The sex didn't come until later when Denise and Cedric got into an argument over him working late nights. Denise said she was so agitated at her husband for not giving her the attention she so desired and that Jamal was there as an attention crutch for her. She didn't realize what was happening until it was too late and they were intertwined in a love sweat embrace. Denise said she was so caught up in Jamal's attentiveness that she lost herself and really didn't think of being married until she was heading home, out of sight out of mind in a sort. She said when she found out she was pregnant everything crashed on top of her all at once and the fear of losing Cedric scared her but not being with Jamal daunted her also. She felt she was caught between who she loved and who she needed was two different people but once she heard her child's heartbeat at her first ultrasound she didn't care about anyone else. She knew it was wrong to have Cedric and his family believe that he was the father of her child but she felt Cedric was more stable financially than Jamal could be for the well-being of her child. When she got caught by Cedric and everyone was looking at her as some sort of harlot, the truth slapped her in the face literally. She told Yolanda that she was more embarrassed that her big sister found out about her infidelities than anyone else and she really wasn't mad but ashamed of it all. Yolanda had let her little sister know she was just disappointed at the whole situation but after she explained everything she will try to understand the calamity she had herself in.

Sherell laid her head on Cedric's chest and his heartbeat seemed to lull her to sleep but she knew she needed to get back home to her son. She started to get out of the bed but Cedric stopped her, "You just gone take my stuff and leave me like that?" "No, but I need to get home to Lamaj", replied Sherell. Cedric wanted her to stay but he understood her responsibilities to her son would always come first and he admired that about her, "I wish I would have gave us a chance a long time ago." Sherell smiled as she got dressed, "Well we can make up for loss time" and kissed him so that it felt like she would never leave if she didn't get up off his bed. Cedric walked her outside to her car and the two had one last passionate embrace before Sherell got in, "I'll call you tonight after Lamaj goes to sleep." Cedric watched as she backed out of the driveway and drove down the street. Sherell couldn't believe the event that just took place as she headed home. A glowing smile wouldn't leave her face as butterflies filled her stomach, "I can't believe we just did that. What the…how the hell did that just happen?" She was confused and joyed all the same but in the back of her mind she started to overthink the situation. Sherell's mind began to churn with scenarios of Cedric using her as a rebound relationship or even getting back with his wife but that all went away with one text when she got home, "I know you just left but I needed to tell you this. I've made many mistakes and foolish decisions in my life. But not being with you thirteen years ago has been my biggest of them all. You have always been there for me even when I wasn't there for myself. You have been a factor in my life that I have taken for granted and I refuse to let you get away this time. Sherell Marie White, I know you are gonna laugh at me and probably tell me to shut up but I am truly falling for you. We don't have to make anything official or claim one another, we can take our time. I just want to be in your presence for as long as you would have me be. I need you in my life." At that moment all of her anxieties of "what ifs" simply went away and she knew they were distend to work it all out in the end. Sherell sat on her bed contemplating what her response could be after reading Cedric's text and Lamaj walked in, "Mama, dad sent me a pic of my little sister, she's so cute and she was born two days ago." The news was a complete gut punch to Sherell's reality right now as she wondered how this will all play out. Her first commitment is her son and she knows that when he finds out who the mother is of his little sister it is going to jolt his core. Sherell even considered just telling him right then but then that would involve telling him about the split up between Cedric and Denise. She was truly stuck with keeping this secret from her son until it was the right time but when is the right time to tell your son that his father was partial cause of a marriage falling apart. Sherell just smiled and watched her son walk away, a proud big brother, looking at his baby sister's picture. She then wondered if Cedric knew that Denise had her baby but she didn't want to say anything to upset him. After getting out of the shower, Sherell got comfortable in her bed and called Cedric, "Hey, sorry I didn't call when I got home but a sister had to take a shower cause somebody had me all sweaty earlier." Cedric laughed, "You the one hat kept speeding up like you was running a race, I was trying to take it slow."

"Boy, it's either go hard or go home. You better catch up or hold on for the ride", replied Sherell. The two laughed and stayed on the phone, for what felt like hours, enjoying one anothers conversation. Cedric felt a feeling he haven't had in a very long time and he didn't want it to end. He had a connection he and Denise lost a long time ago but did nothing to resolve the problem. Cedric assumed working hard and being financially stable was the key to a happy home but he realized that was a false truth. He was able to give his wife almost anything she wanted, cars, trips, money, clothes and jewelry but fell short on what she needed. Cedric made a promise to himself that he's going to work harder for his relationship this time. Sherell really didn't know what to expect from this newly evolving relationship but one thing she did know is that she and Cedric have always worked well together, as a team.

Yolanda walked thru her front door to the smell of dinner being prepared. She entered the kitchen to the sight of Kareem slicing a cucumber for a salad, "Baby, what are you doing? You been busy with the shop all day. You didn't have to cook dinner." Kareem just smiled, "And you been ripping and running all day, this is the least I can do. Now take this glass and go relax while I throw the finishing touches on this here." Yolanda just obeyed orders, took her glass of wine to the dinning room table and relaxed her feet. Shortly after Kareem walked in with a restaurant quality ready meal that consist of grilled salmon, garlic asparagus spears, rice pilaf, honey glazed croissants and a chef salad. Yolanda was amazed at the meal but more than that appreciative of the gesture he just made. Kareem sat down, they said grace and he began asking Yolanda about her day and her visit with Denise. She told him about how her and Denise dissolved their issues with one another after a long talk on what brought on the whole situation. Kareem stayed attentive to Yolanda's every word as she poured out her feelings on the matter only giving his key point of view when prompted to. After Yolanda finished her meal, Kareem got up and put the plates away but came back with sealed envelop with Yolanda's name on it. With the raise of one eyebrow asked Yolanda, "What's this?" "Only one way to find out", replied Kareem. She opened the envelop to find two keys on a key ring and a note that reads, "Please don't take it as these keys resemble the keys to my heart because they're not. These are the keys to my house cause I want you to have full access to me at all times. I want you to be able to come and go as you please but I want you there with me all the time. I know we're just getting good and started but I can't see myself without you in it, I can't go a day without seeing that beautiful face and I refuse to let you go. You nurture me in a way that I can't explain but the feelings you bring when you smile are intense, the joy you bring when you laugh is intoxicating, when you cry I ache and when you love I embrace it like a flower takes in sunlight. Like I said please don't take these keys as a resemblance of the keys to my heart because you had possession of my heart at our first conversation." Yolanda sat on her man's lap, kissed him and they didn't have to say one word to one another because they both knew they were meant for each

other.

Author page:

Ralph M. Edgerson Jr was born and raised in New Orleans, La. He was first encouraged to write by his High School English teacher who saw a true talent in him. Ralph played around with poems and short stories for fun but never anything serious. It wasn't until after surviving Hurricane Katrina with his family that he started to use writing as a sense of release and therapy. He made a home in Katy, TX and Ralph's main focus is family but he writes from the heart about family, love, hurt, joy and pain.

Contact Information

Ralph Edge Edgerson – Facebook

19edge73 – Instagram

r.edgerson73@yahoo.com

rbedge73@gmail.com

decisions-the-series.jimdofree.com

Publisher – Vantage Point Publishing/Dawn Blanchard 317-418-2076

These Decisions are subconscious choices determined thru a lengthy
journey of adjustments.

The stage was set with perfected purpose unknowingly making its host
reluctant.

Make your move. No no no. MAKE YOUR MOVE! While keeping the
Devil in you silent.

Never reveal to your opponent your next advance but don't try to hide it.

See the exceptions to the rules are simply laid out for you as a guide.

But the true investment is knowing when these facts are true or when that
muthafucka lied.

I won't, I couldn't, I can't be your conductor cause it's pointless to tell you
how to move.

The Rook takes the Bishop and the Pawn takes the Knight because it has a
point to prove.

L-shaped angles lead to straight away moves in all directions.

Focus on your grace delegated by your crown of afflictions.

The wrong pass could defeat your clan in an immeasurable faith.

Check One! Check Two!.......Checkmate